The Five Firm Friends – Edith, Cordelia, A   are five sassy career women who confront life head-on. But when Beauty suddenly becomes ill and, after six short weeks, passes away, their world is thrown into confusion. On her deathbed Beauty begs Amanda to promise her one thing – that she and the rest of the FFF will not waste their lives as she has done. All because of an unfaithful husband . . . "Ukhule," she begs of Amanda. May you live a long life, and may you become old.

Beauty's Gift is a moving tale of how four women decide to change their own fate as well as the lives of those closest to them. This is Sindiwe Magona at her very best – writing about social issues, and not keeping quiet. Speak up, she says to women in Africa. Stand up, and take control of your own lives.

Sindiwe Magona

Beauty's Gift

To Jess

Thanks for your support. I hope the book (reading it) will add to the magic of Chautauqua!

Best Wishes

Magona

July 2009

Kwela Books

Kwela Books,
an imprint of NB Publishers,
40 Heerengracht, Cape Town, South Africa
PO Box 6525, Roggebaai, 8012, South Africa
www.kwela.com

Cover design by Hanneke du Toit
Cover image by Christina Richards, Corbis, Great Stock
Author photograph by Simone Scholtz
Typography by Nazli Jacobs
Set in Caslon by Nielfa Cassiem-Carelse
Printed and bound by Paarl Print,
Oosterland Street, Paarl, South Africa

First edition, first impression 2008

ISBN-10: 0-7957-0272-8
ISBN-13: 978-0-7957-0272-3

In memory of my loving son,
Sandile Soyiso Sayedwa.
In my heart, you will
always live, Rwaadibles!

Death is the mother of beauty; hence from her,
Alone, shall come fulfillment to our dreams
And our desires.

WALLACE STEVENS

1

Morning, 28 September 2002
CEMETERY, NY 5, GUGULETHU

God knew the African woman was going to have a very, very hard life. That is why He gave her skin as tough as Mother Earth herself. He gave her that tough, timeless skin so that her woes would not be written all over her face, so that her face would not be a map to her torn and tattered heart.

These were Amanda's thoughts as her eyes came to rest on Mamkwayi's face. Mamkwayi, Beauty's mother, was perched precariously on a white plastic chair, on the family dais, right across from where Amanda stood on legs too numb to feel.

"Amen!" the priest boomed authoritatively, causing Amanda's eyes to stray from the object of her pity.

"Amen!" the other mourners responded.

Next, Nosisa, Hamilton's eldest sister, spoke of Beauty's illness. She'd helped Mamkwayi – who could not speak at her own daughter's funeral – nurse Beauty.

She was brief.

"We hardly had time to get used to the fact that she was ill before she was gone," she began. "She was stolen away from us."

There was a pause and a barely perceptible shake of her head. Then, her voice dropping, she continued, "We didn't see she was going . . . till . . ."

She stumbled over her words, wiping away a tear, before continuing with renewed resolve. "When we saw the illness was getting the upper hand, we rushed her to the hospital. But it was too late. The TB had already advanced to such a stage . . . We brought her home. She wanted to come home . . ."

Again she stopped, and bowed her head.

A hymn rose from the choir.

Amanda let her eyes wander back to the woman she so admired, the woman for whom she sorrowed. How serene Mamkwayi looks, she thought, as a great tenderness welled up from deep inside her. How she didn't die from sheer grief, how she lived through the ordeal of watching her child, her only daughter, die – die such a long, painful death – was a source of wonder to Amanda. It had seemed to drag on for so long, but now that she thought about it Beauty's illness could not have lasted more than six weeks, if that.

Amanda's musings came to an abrupt end as Reverend Mananga announced the next item on the programme. Amanda knew what was coming. And this knowledge changed the tenor of her thoughts.

The sight of the tall man who stepped forward, looking as though he'd just stepped out of *GQ*, infuriated Amanda. Look at him, she thought. Just look how he is all dressed up!

Amanda watched as Hamilton made his way to the head of the grave. The beige silk suit and brown suede shoes went well with the widower's towering physique – he stood head and shoulders above the rest of the men in the cortege. A little self-consciously, he flashed the easy smile that so became his broad mocha face. Hamilton bowed and cleared his throat, then he looked up and his deep-set eyes, bright with unshed tears, slowly swept over the crowd.

In waves, gradually, a hush fell. Now the crowd waited with him, for him.

Even Amanda was affected by the hush. She took in the commanding presence that had brought it about. To think she had loved this man once. Loved him as a friend, loved him like a brother – after all, he had been her best friend's boyfriend and then her husband. Why, she had been the chief bridesmaid at their wedding. And, in the early days, it was to her Hamilton had turned when at a loss regarding a special gift, or when cooking up a surprise for Beauty. They had had such fun together, just the three of them, but these days she had nothing but loathing for Hamilton.

Amanda's eyes again travelled to Beauty's mother. Poor Mamkwayi! But her careful scrutiny of Mamkwayi's face revealed only a calm that seemed as if it were her birthright. The woman is a saint, Amanda thought. Why is it Hamilton who is alive? Why is Beauty dead while her playboy husband lives?

Hamilton began. He read:

Light of my Soul

In shards, my world lies at my feet.
How will I go on? How read the signs,
You no longer by my side?
All joy has fled; my world, shrunk.
Light left my soul. Queen among women.
The chosen. Beloved.

In my heart, you live
Though the long, sunless day
Of your absence would reign.
Though all here proclaim you ...

Amanda couldn't bear to listen to him for another second. Clear as a bell, Hymn 100 poured from her throat, rudely interrupting Hamilton's recital. In the whole of the Anglican hymnal, Beauty had loved that hymn best of all.

Ndakugqala umnqamlezo,
Afa kuwo uMsindisi,
Sendilahla yonk' indyebo.
Ndilidele ikratshi lam!

She sang the first line all alone, but by the time she began the second line, the other three remaining members of the FFF – the Five Firm Friends – were singing right along with her. And by the middle of that line, the whole congregation had joined in. It is customary to stop a long sermon or tedious talk by starting a hymn.

Hamilton dithered. He seemed uncertain whether to continue or wait till the singing stopped.

But the singing did not stop.

Mandingaqhayisi, Nkosi.
Kungengamnqamlezo wakho;
Konke endikuthandayo
Ndikuncame ngenxa yakhe.

Then someone tapped him lightly on the elbow, indicating he should return to his seat, as the priest wanted to continue with the service.

Hamilton glowered at Amanda as he made his way back to his seat. Amanda stared right back, a silent message of loathing passing between the two of them.

The service resumed. Then, just before the casket was lowered, four young men in overalls arrived, carrying bags of cement, buckets and spades – things that looked distinctly out of place at a funeral. Everyone was quite astounded. They set to work even as the service continued. *Shlap-shlap, shlap-shlap* – the sound of cement being mixed enveloped the mourners. When they were right and ready, the team sloshed bucketfuls of wet cement into the grave. Two stood at the edge, overseeing operations from that vantage point, while two jumped into the hole. The latter, in black gumboots, spread the mixture evenly across the bottom and lower walls of the grave.

Once the casket had been lowered onto the wet concrete, the priest threw in a handful of soil. The immediate family was next, starting with Hamilton, holding his son, Sandile, by the hand, followed by Beauty's parents and then the rest of the family.

Benediction followed, and the dismissal soon thereafter.

Immediately, the hordes scattered. Most left the graveside with unseemly haste, scuttling to abandon Beauty to the place of sorrow. In the grip of unforgiving pain, Amanda sensed rather than saw the unravelling of the knots of people all around her.

Let them leave, she thought. She would never leave. Never! She would never leave Beauty all alone. Leaving would be the final acceptance that she was gone.

13

There she stood, tears gushing down her unguarded cheeks. She swayed this way and that, a lone reed midstream during a gale.

"Oh, Beauty!" the cry tore out of her.

* * *

The Gugulethu cemetery, like the township whose name it bears, sprawls unattractively. Here and there a well-kept grave catches the eye, one that shows signs of regular visits by the living, but for the most part the cemetery is a jumble of time-wrought decay, neglect and plain thoughtlessness.

Saturdays, the day usually reserved for funerals, are feasting days for the goats of Section 4, Gugulethu. As she stood there, Amanda knew the goats would surely come to Beauty's grave; death would come swiftly to the wreaths piled high on top of the fresh mound. Expensive and beautiful, they would not see the sun rise the next day.

Amanda tasted gall. She had failed Beauty. She had failed her miserably. Why had she been so timid? Why had she not confronted Beauty with her suspicions?

A hand fell lightly on her right shoulder. That would be Edith, the most caring of the group.

As she turned she saw Cordelia, Doris and Edith standing just behind her, forming a solid line of support. Cordelia and Edith, short but ample, stood a little in front of Doris, as slight in build as Amanda, but a little shorter. Attractive women, their good taste revealed by the subdued funeral clothing they wore.

Amanda drew in a sharp breath. Her shoulders rose high and then slowly sank back to rest. The tallest of the four, she held on to her composure, her slanted eyes burning like dark coals of despair above the prominent cheekbones that linked her to some forgotten Khoikhoi ancestor.

Again, her attention turned to the flowers piled on her friend's grave, wreaths that the goats would devour before the sun set. Slowly, without knowing that she did so, she shook her head.

If Amanda was angry at herself, she felt murderous towards Hamilton. There wasn't the slightest doubt in her mind that he was the cause of Beauty's death. "That dog!" she said, her voice hard.

Covering her mouth with a trembling hand, she fell onto her knees. Lovingly, she patted the raw mound. "Sithandwa, I don't know how we will go on without you . . ." she murmured softly.

Both hands on the fresh ground, she let her head drop until it looked as though she were about to kiss the wet sand. But her shoulders told another story. They heaved and trembled as the sighs that tore out of the depths of her body grew stronger.

Gradually, the sobs dried up, and for a long moment there was silence as Amanda continued kneeling at the foot of Beauty's grave. The others let her be. Silently, they waited. Waited till, finally, she rose.

"Sleep well, sithandwa!" she whispered. "We will be back soon!" Then, with a bitter little smile, she added, "For your birthday . . ." But her voice caught in her throat.

* * *

15

Silently, the four women made their way out of the cemetery. Other funerals were still in progress and clusters of mourners in dark attire dotted the place, some arriving while others departed.

"How can people throw away their loved ones like this?" Edith suddenly said as they approached the cemetery gate.

"Throw away?" asked Doris.

"Come and bury them here and then never pay attention to the graves!"

Doris looked at the neglected graves they were passing. "No respect," she said.

They reached the gate. The street beyond was jammed with traffic, filled with people making their way to and from funerals. To reach the other side of the street, where they'd left their car, the foursome had to dodge their way amongst the unruly taxis and other vehicles that thronged the road.

Amanda and Doris reached the car first and waited for the other two. It was Cordelia's car, and she had the keys. The other three had left their cars at Amanda's Gugulethu home, in NY 74.

Amanda sucked her teeth, suddenly overwhelmed by the day's events.

Doris understood how Amanda felt. "Beauty didn't deserve this . . ." she began.

"Mmffxcmm!" Amanda sucked her teeth again.

"How . . . how could we lose her like this?" Doris asked her friends as Edith and Cordelia made it to the car. "How is it that we didn't see this coming?"

"And how do we go on without her?" Cordelia asked.

Amanda covered her face with both hands. She was weeping, the others knew. Since Beauty had died, the others had marvelled at Amanda's composure. She was, after all, Beauty's best friend. Now they were afraid that she would unravel.

"Hush, Amanda, hush!" Edith said, gently patting her on the back. "You've been so brave all along, don't crumble now."

2

It had not been a large funeral. Saturday funerals seldom were these days. There were just too many of them. Way, way too many. Despite government pronouncements that the Aids pandemic was not as widespread as some health experts stated, it was obvious that the township cemeteries would soon run out of space. Families were even beginning to open old graves and bury new corpses over the long dead.

In the midst of the economic hardship afflicting the country – biting hardest on the forever economically disadvantaged – the fastest-growing industry was firmly rooted in the townships. Business had never been brisker for the undertakers.

And those in the townships seemed bent on affirming death with everything at their disposal. Families went out of their way to outdo one another in the extravagance with which they buried their dead. Coffins were far from cheap, but now people were buying caskets, and choosing the most expensive ones too. Then there was the food and hiring the tent in which the wake would be held, not to mention hiring pots, dishes, crockery, cutlery, benches and chairs.

A few enlightened religious leaders spoke out against this profligacy.

In a newspaper article, Anglican Archbishop Ndungane had publicly begged his priests to guide their parishioners so they would desist from incurring burdensome debts to pay for funerals. Failing that, he urged priests to consider refusing to officiate at such inordinately costly ceremonies. But disposing of the dead in a fitting manner is a sacred undertaking in any society, and now that the Aids pandemic had reversed the order of things, parents – in their grief, their bewildered and confounded sorrow – were giving their children the funerals they had hoped to get from them.

A man of substance, Hamilton was not to be outdone in burying his beloved. Even his detractors admitted he had given Beauty umngcwabo womhlaba.

Beauty's parents had wanted to contribute toward the funeral, but Hamilton refused their offers of help. "I'll take care of everything!" he had said, shutting them out of all the funeral arrangements. "After all, she was *my* wife!"

A man of style, Hamilton had buried Beauty in a dazzling ivory casket with gleaming gold handles – top of the range. The hearse was a white Mercedes-Benz limousine, and behind it, family and close family friends followed in a gleaming fleet of ten white Mercedes-Benz cars.

But not one of Beauty's close friends was in those cars. They remembered how tight-fisted Hamilton had been with her, how all her money had been spent on her family's needs, and how she'd often gone without the things she'd wanted or needed because he spent his own money on wine and women and the other things a womaniser's lifestyle demanded. They also remembered how, eventually, Beauty had learnt to make do without his money. And so they bluntly refused to ride in the convoy. Instead, they had all piled into Cordelia's white BMW.

Theirs was the last car back from the cemetery.

All the mourners were already in the yard, most of them inside the tent. Family, close friends and dignitaries would be inside the house.

Outside the fence, four plastic basins sat on the ground, two on each side of the gate. These basins held water so that those returning from the graveyard could wash their hands and thus leave death and all things pertaining to it outside the gate.

Four basins. But without hesitation, without consultation, the four women made a beeline for the two red ones to the right.

Beauty had been buried in red – a custom-made robe making an unforgettable slash of scarlet in the soft, cushiony white satin inside the gleaming ivory casket. Red, crowned with the thick jet-black of Beauty's locks. To the very end, her hair had stayed amazingly alive around the gaunt wasteland of her face.

Beauty's friends washed their hands and dried them on the towels hanging over the fence. Only then did they enter the yard.

The thronging crowd parted before Beauty's friends. A path opened for them as they went along the stoep and into the house. Everyone present understood that the four young women belonged inside. They were as good as family.

Inside, although the house was packed, people shifted and moved. Four chairs magically materialised and they were soon seated not far from the door.

Mr Mtini, Beauty's father, all dressed up in a black suit, was sitting next to his younger brother, who was speaking, giving words of thanks as expected.

Seeing Beauty's friends enter, the younger Mr Mtini paused till they were seated. When he continued, his voice was loud enough for all to hear, but his words were short on warmth. Those who knew him well wondered what had upset him so much.

"You who know this family will wonder at the absence of the name of our clan brother, Mr Sonti, from the programme. Well, let me enlighten you. I am very sad, very, very sad indeed, to tell you that just as we took our daughter to her last earthly home today, our relatives should also have been taking their son to his place of rest. But because of the close ties between these two families, they are here with us today. Tomorrow, we will be with them."

He paused and looked around, before he continued.

"Yes, our brothers have delayed their own funeral to be with us. And so, our Ceremony of Drinking Water will be with the rise of the sun tomorrow. And as soon as we've done that, we will go to our other home, the home of the Sontis, to lay our son there in his last home. The young man leaves his twin brother so ill that he will not be able to attend the funeral . . . And that is why we thank Sonti, our brother and friend, for being here today, when he leaves behind such a heavy burden at his home . . . a dead child . . . and another very, very ill."

Again he paused, and shook his head.

"We live in terrible, terrible times when relatives are forced to line up funerals, programme them, because more than one home in the same family are busy with the same kind of sad work. The Sonti son was also a teacher. Kuyagwetywa!"

Again he shook his head.

"How else can we explain the inexplicable? What else can we say when the shovel eats the ground with such ferocious frequency? Let us be thankful that our daughter is at peace at last," he said, coming to the end of his delivery.

At once, a woman's voice started, and others quickly joined in singing grace:

> *Nala manzi, aselwayo*
> *Siwaphiwa Nguwe!*
> *Noku kutya, sikutyayo*
> *Sikuphiwa Nguwe!*

But Amanda didn't hear the singing; Mr Mtini's words had reminded her of the thorn-strewn ground they had so lately trodden. Peace? God, what peace? Toward the end, Beauty had had no peace at all. As far as Amanda was concerned, Beauty had just escaped from hell. Her mind spooled back to the moment in time she saw as the beginning of this whole sad mess, when Beauty had bestowed on her such a wonderful gift: "Ukhule!" she had said. "May you grow old!"

3

Saturday, 3 August 2002
THE TOWN HOUSE RESTAURANT, CAPE TOWN
Lunch to celebrate Amanda's thirty-fifth birthday

"Beauty is the limit!" growls Amanda, irritated. "The woman is supposed to be my best friend!"

The outburst creates a wrinkle in the hitherto placid picture the four women make as they sit around a table for five. The empty chair is a fish gap in an otherwise complete mouthful of teeth.

Including the missing Beauty, these are the Five Firm Friends, otherwise known as the FFF: Amanda. Beauty. Cordelia. Doris. Edith. In their early to mid-thirties, the four now waiting are dressed to the nines. Amanda sports a crisp white linen suit, red blouse and a snazzy pair of Charles Jourdan sandals – white with red, blue and green stitching. Doris is, characteristically, in high chops, but they go very well with her slightly flared high-waisted pants and leather jacket. Not much of a dresser, Cordelia is in jeans, but she's jazzed them up with a bright yellow top with red flowers. Only Edith is wearing a skirt. Her husband does not allow her to wear pants, saying that this would offend his parents. Not that Edith minds – she is such a traditionalist herself.

The FFF have known each other since way back when. As friends, they have survived a lot of ups and downs, but today Beauty will be lucky to escape the dressing-down that awaits her at the hands of Amanda.

"She'll be here soon," says Doris absent-mindedly.

"I'll give the flipping so-and-so a piece of my mind!" hisses Amanda, tying away a stray lock.

She and Beauty sport locks. Cord goes short and natural. Edith, like her mother and her mother before her, covers her head. Always, but always! The only difference is that she sometimes wears a beret, whereas they were tied to the doek. Doris is Doris, and how she'll wear her hair on any given day is anybody's guess – she'll wear it natural, twist it, put in a weave, or coil it in some exotic wrap.

"She could have called to tell us she was running late," Amanda continues, calling Beauty on her cellphone.

"Voice mail," she says a moment later, making a rueful face.

The four women console themselves with the thought that Beauty must be on the road, but despite this her unaccustomed lateness makes them all anxious as mother hens with a hawk lurking in the skies.

However, there is nothing to do but wait, so the four friends go back to waiting, silently sipping their drinks.

This is an FFF tradition, a private birthday celebration after the family one. All five prefer the "after", for then they can dissect the family celebration and laugh about the imagination (or lack thereof) of the particular FFF man who happened to be under the microscope on that particular day.

Suddenly, Cordelia's soft, round shoulders shake with suppressed laughter. "Can't bear to leave the matrimonial bliss behind," she says.

The "matrimonial bliss" jab is directed at Hamilton, Beauty's husband. Of all the FFF men, Hamilton is the least liked. Ever since it became clear that he regularly cheats on Beauty, his name has been mud among the other four. He's not the only FFF man who cheats, or has ever cheated, but Mr Man is something else – a repeat offender – and Beauty deserves this least of all. The others call her the heart of the FFF precisely because she is the kindest, the most understanding of them all. Recently, she has been uncommonly punctual, something which the FFF have attributed to Hamilton and her need to put as much distance as possible, as frequently as possible, between herself and the beast. Not that Beauty, sweet and loyal, has ever breathed a word to her friends about her marital problems, but some things are just too hard to hide. And mistresses, young and eager, vying to outdo not just the wife but one another, are hardest to ignore.

Edith glances at her watch. "She must be having baby-sitting problems."

"Pur-lee-z," says Amanda, "the woman has a full-time maid!"

Doris's head jerks up. "'Help', Amanda," she corrects her friend, brows raised.

"Same difference," Amanda retorts. "My mother was a maid. She worked in white people's kitchens, and only stopped when I started working and forced her to quit. Maid! Maid! Maid!"

"Sweetheart," says Doris, with exaggerated patience. "The times, they are a-changing! The politically correct term is 'help' or 'home help'."

"Whatever!" Amanda flicks an impatient hand. For the umpteenth time she looks toward the door. "There's no reason madam isn't here yet, unless that husband of hers has . . ."

"Hamilton, Amanda," interjects Edith. "The man has a name."

"Too big a name, if you ask me!" Amanda says, nose wrinkled.

"Who cares what anyone calls that so-and-so?" Doris asks, rolling her eyes, "fed up" written all over her face.

"Aha!" shouts Cordelia jubilantly. "Speak of the dev–"

She stops short. She, Cordelia, who is never at a loss for words.

All four stare at the approaching figure. The grotesque face that appears in place of Beauty's leaves them all speechless.

"Sithandwa!" Amanda is the first to find her tongue. She leaps up, sending her wooden chair scraping across the marble floor. There is no mistaking the anxiety in her voice.

Beauty smiles. Tries to.

The grimace hits her friends in the pit of the stomach.

"What happened?" asks Amanda as she reaches her.

"Nothing," replies Beauty, brows raised in clear irritation as she avoids Amanda's eagerly outstretched arms.

Gingerly, she lowers herself into the empty seat next to Amanda's.

A furtive look passes between the other three.

Amanda hovers uncertainly. "The rat!" she finally says beneath her breath.

There is a ripple of consternation at the next table, where a young white woman sits with two little children, a girl and a boy, all three shockingly blonde and blue-eyed.

Seeing this, Edith is embarrassed. She is also slightly irritated by Amanda's theatrics. "Utheni? What have you done to yourself?" she asks Beauty, her tone that of a mother talking to a little girl who has grazed her knee.

"Nothing . . . Nothing."

Cordelia harrumphs.

There is a brief silence as each of the FFF tries to grasp the meaning of Beauty's words. Two words. The same word. With the face she brings with her, the words add up to a big fat something. That's how the others see it, and that's how Amanda calls it. "Nothing?" she says, glaring at

Beauty. "When did he do this to you?" The words shoot out like bullets from a gun.

Beauty's brows hitch up north. "No one did anything to me, Amanda," she says, a firm nod accompanying her words. Her voice is icy.

At this, Cordelia groans. Doris and even mild-mannered Edith stare at Amanda and Beauty in disbelief. The two are best friends and the nucleus of the Five Firm Friends. They have been friends longer than all the others. The group came into being around this twosome. There is something special between them, which is why they call each other "sithandwa". Sometimes sparks fly between the two, and the other three are happy to play referee, but this is different.

"Beauty, pur-lee-z," says Amanda, flopping onto her chair and rubbing her clammy palms on her thighs. "You're going to sit there, look me straight in the eye, and lie for that dog?"

"His name is Hamilton," Beauty snaps right back. "And I'm not ly–"

But before she can finish, Amanda jumps down her throat. "Don't! Whatever you do, Beauty, don't fall into the trap of making excuses for your abuser!"

"Women do that all the time," Doris says quietly.

"It doesn't make it right," barks Cordelia, getting in before Beauty.

"But Hamilton didn't do anything to me, I tell you."

"Jaa, right!" Amanda scoffs. "The gods kissed you while you slumbered and you just woke up with your lips all swollen like that?"

"Actually," says Beauty, her brows arched, "if everybody would just let me expl–"

But the words come out all blurred, her raw-steak lips hindering articulation, and again Amanda doesn't let her finish what she is trying to say. Impatiently, she puts up her hand like a traffic cop stopping an errant driver. "I know! I know!" she says, each word thick with scorn. "You bumped into the doorjamb!"

There is a nervous twitter from the group as the other women try to dissipate the tension. They all laugh. All except Beauty. Her bright round eyes brim and the laughter comes to an abrupt end. None of them can remember one of them ever crying long tears because of a sharp remark.

Four pairs of troubled eyes, full of questions, fasten themselves on Beauty. Her friend's tears startle Amanda most of all.

A silence descends upon the group.

"Let's act like the grown women we're supposed to be," Edith says under her breath.

Mute, Beauty looks back at her friends and reads the questions in their faces. Then her eyes busy themselves with inspecting the fingers bunched on her lap. "Please, guys," she pleads, "can we talk about this later?"

Right there, Amanda's heart breaks. God, even what she's wearing is tired. Beauty always wears red. Yes, she might mix and match it with some other colour, but the base of her outfit is always, but always, red. Not today. Today there is more navy than red in her outfit.

"Friends of mine!" shouts Doris, bringing everybody back to the moment. "We're here to celebrate a birthday."

As though on cue, the waitress approaches their table. "Ready now?" she asks cheerily.

* * *

Celebrating is the furthest thing from the minds of the FFF as the group reaches Amanda's Gugulethu home. This is standard practice. Most of the gang's outings wind up at this place, where they can be themselves with absolutely no inhibitions. But now, all the joviality of before is gone. Throughout the half-hour car journey, the same thoughts have been preying on the mind of each member of the FFF. And now each of them wants to talk about Beauty and her appearance. There is just no way they can pretend she doesn't look the way she does. Each woman has questions. But these are questions each is too afraid to ask.

However, no sooner are they inside the house than the FFF give Beauty a look that says, "Out with it!"

Beauty flops onto the nearest chair and, for a moment, closes her eyes and cups her face in one hand, so that the swollen lips are out of sight. She seems at rest, draws a deep breath. Then, without opening her eyes, she speaks.

"For two weeks," she says slowly, her voice hushed, "I woke up each morning with these swollen lips . . . and a little swelling around the eyes." She stops, lifting her eyes to her friends.

Silently, they look back. No one says a word.

"But then it all disappeared again, and for days it wasn't there," Beauty continues. "And now, suddenly, it's back."

For a while, no one speaks as each woman digests this new and unfamiliar piece of information.

"Been to the doctor?" Edith asks eventually.

Beauty shakes her head and says the swelling doesn't hurt.

"Looks awful, girlfriend," Cordelia says, and chuckles.

At that, the mood lightens and Beauty's smile grows bolder, although her unnaturally thickened lips make a grimace of her usually dazzling smile.

A few more questions follow. Beauty answers them all with studied patience. Then, shaking her head, she puts up a hand: "Hey, enough about me and my stupid face," she says cheerily. "What wishes has everybody brought our darling 'Manda?"

No one wants to go first – each woman wants her wish to be the best, wants to hear what the others say first, so she can try and top it. However, someone has to start the ball rolling.

"Well, then," says Cordelia finally, "here's to happiness!"

"Health and wealth!" is Doris's contribution.

Edith takes Amanda's hand in hers and clasps it tightly. "May you never take a faulty step," she says. "And if you do, may you swiftly find your way back to your true path." She gives the hand a small, quick squeeze.

Beauty smiles.

Tries to.

Her wish for her best friend is briefly put.

"Ukhule!"

Amanda feels a lump form in her throat. Ukhule, Beauty, she thinks. May you grow old too!

A makoti showed the FFF to the main bedroom, where, as expected, Mamkwayi was in semiseclusion, with only a few relatives and close friends in attendance.

Flanked by two older women, Mamkwayi sat on a chair – the first step in the healing process. Even though a heavy woollen shawl was draped over her shoulders and she wore a black doek on her head – the dress code of the newly bereaved – her black frock had been exchanged for a blue German-print skirt and matching apron, a navy cardigan completing the outfit.

That mattress on which she'd sat all through the wake period was up against the wall now. Leading up to the funeral all the furniture, including the bed, had been removed from the room. The furniture would only be returned to its proper place the following day. In fact, everything would return to its place now that Beauty had been buried. Now life at 8 Mnga Street could return to some semblance of normality. But that would only start the next day, after the family had been made to drink water – ukusezwa amanzi.

"Come in! Come in!" Mamkwayi said, waving the young women in. A small, sad smile played at the corners of her mouth.

Just then, Beauty's brother, Mpumelelo, stepped into the room through the other door, clippers in hand. His own head had already been shaved. Three children followed him – a boy and two little girls – all sporting clean-shaven heads. The boy was Sandile, Beauty's son. The girls were Mpumelelo's daughters, Nkosazana and Nolitha. Mpumelelo hugged each of the FFF.

Sandile kissed Mamkwayi on the cheek, then made a beeline for Auntie Ama and his other FFF aunties for hugs and kisses.

It was then that Mpumelelo remembered why he'd come. "Mama, are you ready?" he asked.

"What, now?" Mamkwayi queried.

"When would you like me to do it?"

"Hayi, bhuti," she said, smiling. "Come back when our friends here have left. You think I want everyone looking at my head, full of white hair as it is?"

Everybody chuckled – tentative little laughs. Mamkwayi was being very brave, showing the people who had come to grieve with her that she had gained strength from them, from their support and their prayers.

"You're right, Mamkwayi," said the bottle-legged woman who sat on her left. "We would all be shocked . . . we never thought a spring chicken like you would have a single grey hair on her head!"

More laughter followed and Mamkwayi relented. "Well, come on, then," she said, and took off her doek.

As Mpumelelo began to shave her head, Mamkwayi remembered her daughter's friends. "You must get something to eat," she said, her head bent forward under the clippers. "Do you want to go to one of the tables? Or to the room with the other teachers? Which is it going to be, zintombi?"

But there was no way the FFF would go to eat at any table. Not today. Not here. What if they found themselves sharing a table with Hamilton? Moreover, they had other pressing business to attend to before sunset.

Politely, they declined the invitation.

"We just wanted to see you, Mama, before we left," Amanda said, speaking for all of them.

The FFF planned to spend the rest of the day remembering Beauty, honouring her and consoling one another as best as they knew how. No men (they could take care of themselves). No children (Amanda's brother PP and his wife were taking care of the whole FFF brood). The four women wanted to be alone with their memories of Beauty.

"Imkil' itshomi yenu – Your friend has left," said Mamkwayi, standing up and brushing the hair off her shoulders, head and breast.

She surveyed the clumps of hair at her feet, her lips tight. Then she sat down again, sinking deeper into her chair, shrinking a little as Mpumelelo carefully began to clip away the last few tufts he'd missed.

"Kodwa, ze ningasilahli, zintombi zam! – But you, daughters, do not forsake us!" Mamkwayi said, reminding the FFF that she would be seeing them the next day, when they would all drink water together before going to the Sonti funeral.

Again, a little tearful, the young women hugged Mamkwayi.

"Thank you, my children. You really loved this friend of yours," said Mamkwayi as she tied her doek back onto her head.

"We love her still," said Doris.

* * *

"You know," Cordelia said into the silence that had once again settled over the FFF as they drove back to Amanda's Gugulethu home, "I half expect girlfriend to appear suddenly and laugh her head off, telling us, 'Got you all – Ndinifumene! I just wanted to see how much you all love me. I am most certainly not dead!'"

"Remember how well she looked the last time we were all out together?" Amanda asked.

Cordelia did. And so did the others. They all remembered how perfectly normal and healthy Beauty had looked the last time she was out with them, at Didi Ngambu's place in Montana Village. Doris had invited them to a book discussion group, where they'd discussed "Sunday Morning", a poem by an American poet whose name they no longer recalled.

And Doris also remembered how much the poem had upset Beauty. Had she already known that she was not well? "We should have known something was not right," she said. "The way she reacted, how everything upset her that day – that should've told us something!"

"Fact is, we did not know she . . ." Amanda left her sentence unfinished.

"That was the very last time she was with us in public . . ." said Edith.

"But we didn't know it then," said Cordelia. "Didn't know she was leaving us . . . *Would* be leaving us," she quickly corrected herself. As though tense made the slightest difference to the awful outcome.

5 | *11 August 2002*
JANEY CLOSE, MONTANA VILLAGE

"Didi is ditzy," grumbles Doris as she parks her car outside the yellow-brick house in Janey Close.

The woman only sent her the poems for discussion the previous day. Doesn't give a body much time to do any reading, she fumes silently, what a waste of time this is going to be. Her thoughts fly to the FFF. Her friends are going to kill her. She owes all of them for agreeing to come to this. The FFF aren't particularly keen readers, and they had only reluctantly agreed to come to the discussion group now and then to give her support.

The discussion group meets once a month, always on the second Sunday of the month, always at the home of the woman who proposed the book to be discussed. At the previous meeting, Didi came up with Wallace Stevens, an American poet no one had ever heard of. She brought enough copies of the poem "Sunday Morning" for the others and said she would e-mail them other examples from the collection.

"She should've done it weeks ago," Doris again grumbles to herself as she grabs her bag.

She sees Cordelia's car. That tells her she is definitely the last of the

FFF to arrive. Cordelia was bringing Amanda, Beauty and Edith. Doris gives a little chuckle. She knows she'll get it in the neck from her friends, dragging them to this and then arriving last.

She makes her way up onto the stone stoep. Voices. Laughter. They should be starting soon.

And, sure enough, as soon as Doris seats herself, the meeting is called to order.

One woman complains about doing an obscure American poet's works "when there is so much good poetry, right here at home".

Thereafter, the discussion comes to life. Doris says the poem is about woman power and sexuality, while Edith thinks it is a religious poem, promising real liberation after death. Someone else thinks it speaks of a new democratic order – that is what the word "green" suggests to her.

"Green could also mean unseasoned, inexperienced," says Cordelia.

But Nokuthula, a lawyer, like Doris, replies that, to her, "green" suggests everlastingness. That, taken together with the words "holy hush" and "ancient", the poem could be seen to recall biblical themes such as eternity and creation. "Certainly, if we call ourselves Christians," she says, "this poem should speak to us. We are born into death and we die into life . . . When we leave this earth it is not the end of us. We are but in another form, occupy another space."

Nokuthula is a born-again Christian, a member of the Universal Church or some such.

They are all surprised when Beauty voices her unhappiness, claiming that the poem seems to suggest fulfilment only through death.

Something about the vehemence with which Beauty says this makes Doris look at her, really look at her. And that is when Doris decides she is being alarmist. Any old fool can see nothing is the matter with Beauty, she tells herself, nothing at all.

The discussion of "Sunday Morning" takes up so much time that the poem ends up being the only one the group discusses.

"See, I don't know why one would say Stevens's work is too Western," says Doris, winding up the discussion. "After all, beneath the superficial envelope of skin, we are all the same: heir to the same aspirations, emotions and foibles."

"That is so-o true," says Didi, all smiles, as if she's just been granted a birthday wish.

"True or not," says Beauty, standing up and tucking in her scarf, "I've got to go!"

She hurriedly buttons the light woollen jacket she has on, hugs Amanda and leaves.

Amanda gathers Beauty explained her premature exit to the other members of the FFF. A nod from Cordelia confirms her suspicions. But how is she getting home? As if she has read her mind, Cordelia plucks two or three times at her chin with her thumb and forefinger, indicating that Hamilton is picking Beauty up.

* * *

"They're off to Goudini," Cordelia tells Amanda after the meeting.

"Goudini? Where the heck is that?"

"Posh spa other side of Paarl, my dear," Cordelia says, handing Amanda one of the pamphlets Beauty gave her earlier.

The trip is Hamilton's belated Women's Day present. He'd been away on a business trip on the day itself. The Goudini Spa is his way of making it up to Beauty.

"In fact," Edith adds, "Beauty is driving out there in a posh, brand-new car."

"Hamilton's gift," Doris says, smiling wryly.

"He must feel helluva guilty," is all Amanda can bring herself to say.

A little peeved Beauty hasn't told her of her plans, Amanda puts her oversight down to the pressure of Hamilton, the errant hubby, suddenly playing lovey-dovey. What is he buying from her this time? And how long will all this attention last? Anyway, she's sure she'll hear about it later in the day. Beauty is sure to call her.

Strangely, though, not only does Beauty not call her, she doesn't answer her cellphone when Amanda calls her later that evening. Amanda tries again the next morning. And again the same thing happens – Beauty's cellphone seems stuck on voice mail.

Of course, Hamilton comes first, Amanda tells herself, quelling her irritation. After all, I am just a friend and Hamilton is family, the father of Beauty's child, the man Beauty married.

* * *

In the days that follow, none of the FFF are able to reach Beauty.

When, thinking that the lovebirds should be back home, Amanda finally phones Beauty on her land line, Hamilton is the one to pick up. It is the same the day after, and the day after that, and every time he says that

Beauty can't come to the phone – she's in a meeting, they have visitors, she's resting.

Although she's cheesed off, Amanda assumes that the lovebirds are playing truant from work, taking time out for themselves – stranger things have happened. The whole thing is annoying, but the romantic in her can't help being happy for her friend.

Then, a little over a week after the book discussion in Montana Village, Mamkwayi calls Amanda. Amanda can't remember the last time Mamkwayi called her. So when she gets the call, and late too, she knows immediately that something is wrong.

It is.

Very, very wrong.

"Beauty is not well," Mamkwayi says sombrely. "From the GF Jooste Hospital we brought her straight here, so I can care for her. A man cannot look after her the way she is."

Amanda quickly learns that Beauty has spent the whole week in hospital. What had happened to her friend's plans? Why had Hamilton lied to her?

"You say she's been in hospital for a week?" she asks.

"Yes," confirms Mamkwayi. "She was discharged today, late this afternoon."

Mamkwayi tells Amanda she is calling her because Beauty is asking for her. And could Amanda please tell the others? Mamkwayi doesn't have to be specific; it is understood that she means the FFF.

The rest of the FFF are just as startled. They put Hamilton's lies down to bad manners. That and conceit. It can't possibly be superstition; the man is far too sophisticated for that. However, they all agree Beauty has to be

39

terribly ill to agree to go home to be nursed by her mother. Beauty dotes on Mamkwayi and she would do almost anything to spare her mother any trouble. And, at Mamkwayi's age, there couldn't possibly be a more troublesome chore than having to care for a sick person.

At the crack of dawn the next day, Amanda, Cordelia, Doris and Edith descend on 8 Mnga Street, unaware that this is just the first of several visits they will pay their friend over the next six weeks.

6 | *28 September 2002*
NY 74, NO. 200, GUGULETHU

To the far west of Gugulethu the sun had begun to turn Table Mountain a brilliant golden hue, but down on the Cape Flats, Gugulethu went about its usual business, still basking in the late-afternoon sun.

Edith broke the silence that had fallen as the car made its way south toward NY 74. "I'm glad that Hamilton agreed to have the funeral at her parents' home," she said quietly. When no one responded, she added, her voice suddenly energised, "Did you see that casket?"

"He certainly spared no cost," Doris scoffed.

"Beauty appreciates it, I'm sure," Cordelia said, her voice cold. "All this finery, this masquerade . . . Hell, for what?" She paused, glared at Edith, and growled, "Is it going to bring Beauty back?"

Edith hunched her shoulders.

Cordelia shook her head. "And cement!"

"To prevent thieves from 'recycling' the casket," said Doris.

Edith found her tongue again. "What has come over our people?" she lamented. "To steal from the dead!"

Doris had had enough. To change the subject, she said, "You must agree, though, that the poem he read was straight from the heart."

"Bullshit!" Cordelia shot back. "That dog doesn't have a heart. All that glittering extravagance was to salve his conscience!"

Amanda was relieved to hear Cordelia's blunt assessment. It showed that she wasn't the only one who had had doubts about Hamilton's performance.

Again they drove on in silence. The car turned off NY 1 into NY 50. They were less than a minute away from their destination.

Of the married members of the FFF, only Amanda still had a township house. Edith and Beauty had moved straight from their parents' homes to suburbia after they had married, and Cordelia had sold her Gugulethu house to raise a deposit on her suburban home. But Amanda and her husband, Zakes, had had enough between them, and she had not had to sell her house in order to buy the house in Muizenberg where they lived with Zingisa, their nine-year-old son.

Amanda loved living in Muizenberg. But, against the wishes of her husband, and in spite of ridicule from family and friends, she had stubbornly refused to give up her Gugulethu house. She didn't see why she should. She'd bought the house long before she was married, and, besides, where else would she perform amasiko – traditional ceremonies?

Off NY 50, Cordelia turned right into NY 68, a blink of a street with eight houses in all – four on either side – and immediately left into NY 74.

A cluster of people greeted the FFF, just outside the gate of Amanda's house, near where, that morning, they had left their cars.

"What is this?" Doris asked.

"Our cars!" Edith croaked worriedly.

Would the time ever come when such questions would no longer be necessary? Amanda wondered. When would the level of crime in the townships drop to normal? Whatever that meant.

Cordelia brought the car to a halt and they all clambered out. The huddle near the gate shifted in order to see the new arrivals. Behind them, exactly where the FFF had left them that morning, their three cars gleamed.

"We're okay," Amanda said, relief evident in her voice.

Amanda turned her attention to her neighbour, now approaching the FFF. This was Thandi, a former teacher, kicked out of two jobs within a year for absenteeism. Her puffy phuza face told the tale. She drank like a fish and could never make it to work on Mondays. When Fridays also became iffy, she got the sack.

"Mmelwane!" Thandi hailed Amanda jovially in her scratchy voice.

Amanda knew several of the people in Thandi's group – the gossip Samantha, Nomsa of the hippo hips and stick legs, and very pregnant Neliswa. The others she knew by sight. There were two men in the group – Moses, a won't-work gooiweg of a man, and Zolile, a policeman. Alcohol was their common denominator; they were all Thandi's drinking buddies.

Thandi reached the FFF. "Glad to see you, Mmelwane!" she chuckled. "You should visit us more often, you know?"

Amanda's neighbours were not at all thrilled that her house was unoccupied most of the time. They said the vacant look of the house encouraged thieves to prowl around, making the whole block vulnerable.

"You'll definitely see more of me during the holidays, Mmeli!" said Amanda as they all crossed the street and reached Thandi's group.

"Do you know the Sonti twins, Lungile and Lunga, teachers who live in NY 1, in Section 3?" Samantha asked by way of welcome.

"*High-school* teachers," Zolile added. "Both had Aids and one has died."

Amanda nodded.

43

She was startled by Zolile's next words. "Do you know whether they . . . uhm" – he chuckled – "did *it* together?"

Amanda was baffled. In her confusion, she frowned.

"He means the twins," Thandi explained.

"Did what together?"

"It . . . you know . . . slept together!"

"Twin to twin," Moses said, and sniggered.

"Yhoo!" Edith gasped. "How *could* they? They are men! Brothers!"

"Maybe they are homosexuals," he added gleefully.

Thandi's group nodded knowingly.

"Homosexuals?" asked Cordelia, her eyebrows arched. "And that gives them Aids, in your opinion? Because heterosexual people don't die of Aids?"

But irony is often lost on people blinded by their own brilliance.

"How else could they both have Aids at the same time?" Moses shouted and his group burst into laughter.

* * *

"Mmffxcmm!" Amanda sucked her teeth in exasperation as soon as they were inside the house.

The FFF had planned to grab a bite as soon as they got to NY 74. Now, however, they found that the disquieting exchange they'd just had with Thandi's friends had taken away their appetite.

"Later, perhaps . . ." Amanda said, covering the plates with other plates and putting a dishtowel over the lot.

"Shall we go on with our business, then?" Doris asked.

But, instead of remembering and honouring Beauty as they'd intended, their minds turned to the conversation with Thandi's drunken friends.

"The pity of it is," said Cordelia with feeling, "there are millions of morons like Moses out there. Millions!"

"Friends of mine," Doris said, laughing, "while we weren't looking, some mean-spirited mlungu cloned clowns like Moses and planted them in our midst!"

"You're damn right!" chortled Cordelia. "No one is born *that* stupid!"

They all laughed.

Suddenly, their spirits lifted, and down memory lane they went, remembering Beauty. Beauty had loved jazz – so did the others. It was one of the many things they shared, a love of jazz played real low. In Beauty's case, however, it had almost been an obsession.

And so, in honour of Beauty, they played Cape Town's favourites, Mankunku Ngozi and Abdullah Ibrahim – and Hugh Masekela, too, although he was a Jozi man.

7 | *Afternoon, 30 August 2002*
8 MNGA STREET, MALUNGA PARK

This day, a Friday, the visit starts just like the others before it. Beauty's wan face lights up at the sound of her friends' voices, hushed though they are.

There is a formula here, a routine. Beauty asks about their children, their jobs, people they all know or have known.

Until her voice grows thin.

Until she closes her eyes and they fear they have exhausted her meagre strength and begin to whisper among themselves.

But today, instead of drifting off to sleep, Beauty clears her throat as if there is something important she wants to say.

Her four friends hush.

Then, to everyone's surprise, Beauty struggles to sit up. Struggles up until she is slouched over the pillow at her knees, or where her knees should be. She's so thin now that there's nothing there. The blankets are flat. Flat till where the feet stick up as though disjointed, things with no link at all to the scrawny neck jutting out from the blankets that are hiding the emaciated stick of a body.

Beauty asks her friends to keep her money in the savings club they formed five years ago, and to let her investment grow until her son reaches the age of twenty-one. Shock silences the four women. They listen as Beauty continues. "But if you see he doesn't need it, if his father has provided well for his education, and Sandile isn't suffering financially, then keep it longer."

"Longer? But why?" Doris asks.

"I'd like to give him the deposit on his first house . . . before or after marriage," she tells them. "Be mothers to our son . . . especially . . ." She pauses, her eyes filling with tears.

"Don't, Beauty! Sithandwa, don't!" Amanda pleads.

Beauty smiles.

Tries to smile.

The effort cracks her lips and they ooze tiny droplets of thin brown blood. The wan smile she manages is a ghost of what it used to be; gaunt dongas have eroded her pretty face.

"Now," she continues, her words coming with great effort. "Especially should my parents no longer be here . . ." She pauses again, her dry lips opening to reveal shrunken gums. She nods. Slowly. Painfully. She nods again.

"Please do not worry yourself on that score," says Doris, while the other three chorus their support.

"You should know," says Amanda, smiling through tears, "you don't even have to ask us to do that, sithandwa."

"I know," she whispers, and slumps back down.

Amanda bends down to kiss her friend on the forehead.

"My parents . . ."

Quickly, Edith steps in. She can see that Beauty is exhausting herself.

"Nothing's going to change," she reassures her. "We'll visit your parents just as though . . ." She finds she cannot go on, she cannot say "as though you were still alive".

"You must live!"

If a cannon had been fired inside that bedroom, the four women could not have been more startled. So powerful is the voice from the bed.

"Wha-at?" squeaks Cordelia.

To everyone's utter amazement, Beauty again struggles to pull herself up onto her elbows. Mesmerised, pity and admiration lancing their hearts, they watch and remember that Beauty, until recently, had been a fitness fanatic, the only one in the group to belong to a gym.

But the valiant struggle is to no avail. Beauty crumples back onto her bed. The skeleton has taken over. Only the voice is strong, as vibrant as before. "Damn you, my friends, if only . . ."

"And this damn visit is over!" a voice barks from just inside the door, interrupting her.

Beauty flinches.

Heads turn.

Impeccable in a double-breasted navy silk suit, Hamilton fills the doorway. Stands there, holding it open, waiting. "Can't you people see she's tired out?" he says, nostrils flaring.

They hadn't heard the door open, hadn't heard Hamilton slink in. Now silence reigns.

Beauty's dimming eyes rove around frantically as she tries to visualise her friends where she has placed them in the room according to their voices.

Hamilton angrily snatches off his sunglasses. Then he repeatedly waves them over his right shoulder, his thumb jabbing the way out.

"We must go," Edith whispers to the others.

"Please come again," says Beauty urgently. "Soon!"

All nod. They nod even though they know she cannot see them. They are too choked up to open their mouths. It is difficult to leave her like this. If only they'd had more time . . . If only Hamilton hadn't come in. A few minutes more and Beauty would have been able to complete what she was on the brink of saying.

If only . . .

They promise to return, to come and see her again. Soon. Soon.

"Soon!" Beauty whispers, turning her head toward the wall.

Amanda knows she is crying.

* * *

From now on, only Amanda is allowed. Hamilton will not permit any of the others to come and see Beauty. "It exhausts her," he says, and will not budge.

Soon after this, Hamilton moves Beauty back "to her own home", against the wishes of her parents, and Mamkwayi is forced to go and nurse her daughter in Hamilton's house, under his supervision.

With the FFF barred from visiting Beauty, it falls upon Amanda to keep the others updated. In the weeks that follow, she loses track of time. Everything blurs.

8 | *Night, 28 September 2002*
NY 74, NO. 200, GUGULETHU

It was getting late. On a day like today, the FFF were more loath to part than usual. They needed to be together to reassure each other that they would make it through this long, dark night, to reassure each other that they would go on living despite what had happened. But it was getting late. So they agreed to meet again at NY 74 at six-thirty the following morning, and to proceed promptly to Malunga Park.

"The body is coming at eleven," Edith reminded everybody.

Beauty's family would leave home for the Sonti funeral a little after ten.

"Please be safe, all of you," Amanda said, seeing her friends out, one after the other.

She waved them off and stood at the gate watching the tail-lights of the three cars disappear, one by one, around the corner of NY 74 and NY 68 – Edith and Cordelia would be driving north, Doris, of course, still lived in Gugulethu with her parents. Still Amanda lingered, admiring the clear African night sky. Was that the Milky Way over there? How she wished she knew more about the constellation. Perhaps she should take an astronomy course at the University of Cape Town's Summer School. That should be affordable even to her – not only in money terms, but time. Ah, well . . .

she'd think about it. There were so many things to do, so little time in which to do them.

Amanda sighed, a deep longing for happier times coming over her. Quickly, she went back to the house and began closing the windows. She locked the back door, put all the food away and made sure all the taps were turned off tightly. Finally, she phoned Muizenberg. There was no reply. The phone just rang and rang and rang. Amanda looked at her watch. Where on earth could Zakes be? Zingisa was with him. Where were they? Finally, she gave up and gathered her things to leave.

On the way out, she switched off the lights.

* * *

The night was clear and crisp, but Amanda's mind was all muddled as she got into her white Tazz and drove away. She couldn't make up her mind which way to go home. She could take a roundabout route, go north on NY 1, past the police station, and leave Gugulethu via the Klipfontein Road. It was safer, to be sure, but the drive towards the police station, along NY 1, was long and lonely, especially this late at night. It would be faster to leave Gugulethu through the south side, the Lansdowne Road side. That way, she'd be out of the township and its many dangers in less than a minute.

Which is why we moved to the suburbs! Out of the blue, she heard those words, often uttered by Zakes, her husband. Words said in puzzled irritation. Zakes only went to the townships for soccer (and the shebeens, although he wouldn't admit to that one). He couldn't see why Amanda kept any link with the township. Sure, she worked there, taught English at Thembelihle, one of the high schools in Khayelitsha. But that didn't mean she had to spend so much time in the accursed place, did it? As for her keeping her house in Gugulethu instead of selling it, well . . . Zakes put that up there with all the other incomprehensible things Amanda did. Like refusing to change jobs when she was offered an opportunity to teach at a school in the suburb in which they lived.

Forget the convenience, her workload would be so much lighter, the facilities available to her so much better!

But Amanda just couldn't do it. She couldn't abandon the African child for greener pastures. She couldn't join the brain drain. She felt guilty enough as it was, running away to live in the relative safety Muizenberg appeared to offer.

Amanda rounded NY 75. To her amazement, the short access path to NY 1 South, opposite the administration buildings, was chock-a-block with traffic, all at a standstill. An ambulance and police cars stood in a knot, lights blazing, bystanders clustered all around.

Amanda asked some of the onlookers what the matter was.

"Accident," said one, brightly.

"Two drivers of amaphela got their cars kissing," said another, enjoying his joke.

"One of them was drunk," yet another added. "The drunk driver has been shot dead. Now the police are looking for the shooter. They say he ran away down NY 72!"

You are certifiable, Amanda. Know that? Certifiable! Amanda heard Zakes's words, as clearly as if he were sitting right beside her. What was she doing alone in Gugulethu in the middle of the night?

Needless to say, by the time she finally got home, it definitely felt like the middle of the night. The streets were totally deserted and the streetlamps looked lonely and sad, the light they shed eerily thin.

When she got to the garage door, leading to the study through which they reached the bedroom, it was locked.

Had Zakes forgotten she was still out?

She glanced at her watch.

A quarter to eleven. The roadblock had cost her the best part of an hour – at least!

Was Zakes annoyed with her because she had not come home earlier? Hell, he stayed out late too. More often than she ever did. Then she remembered. She'd called just before she'd left Gugulethu and he hadn't been home.

In a huff, Amanda made her way out through the side door and into the courtyard, but the front door was double-locked, rendering her latch-key utterly useless. What the hell did he think he was doing, locking her out like this? Now she had to go back through the front gate and ring the bell. Furious, she stomped out and rang the bell long and hard.

That would serve him right.

Instantly, a light came on inside.

He couldn't have been asleep, then. He must have been waiting for her to knock or ring. Well then, she had done just that. She walked back in.

Footsteps.

A moment later, the front door swung open. "Well, well, well! Look who'zh finally home!" Zakes slurred.

"Like you've been home the whole day, waiting for me," Amanda grumbled, pushing past him.

"Where harr've you been?" Zakes asked.

"You know I went to Beauty's funeral." She was still annoyed he had chosen to attend a soccer match instead of supporting her.

Zakes straightened himself, trying to sober up.

Amanda wrinkled her nose, the image of the two mangled cars near the administration offices flashing through her mind. "You know you shouldn't drink and drive," she said, shaking her head, "especially when you have Zingisa with you."

He smiled and, fleetingly, she saw his face become that of the man she had fallen hopelessly in love with.

Impatient with herself, Amanda blinked away the face that swam in front of her and focused on the drunken one instead. She wished Zakes would stop drinking. "Is Zingisa already in bed?" she asked angrily.

* * *

When would she wean herself of the habit? Zingisa was ready. For over a year, he'd been urging her to stop barging into his room. He was not a baby, he had reminded her. Well, she enjoyed the ritual that had started when he *was* a baby – checking in to see that all was well. Later came reading together. They'd had lots of fun, but time had marched on and her son was ready to cut the apron strings. Where had the years gone? She had tried to stop, but in moments of stress, she reverted. She wasn't that bad, she hadn't done this for months, she reminded herself, a sad little smile on her face. She took one flung-out arm and held onto the hand, then tenderly put it against her cheek. Warm. Her eyes went to his face, such a faithful replica of his father's. She prayed her son took only his physical qualities from his father.

Immediately, she corrected herself – she was not being quite fair to her husband. Zakes was not a bad man. In fact, he was a damn good man. He liked his drink a little too much, perhaps, but he was not a bad man. Her marriage had had many ups and downs, but at least Zakes only had the one child – Zingisa – and that with her, his lawfully wedded wife. No, Zakes's only flaw was the drinking – going to the shebeen, losing track of time and coming home soused. But that was the case with most men she knew. They went there with their friends. It was a male thing. Compared to womanisers like Hamilton, the man was a saint. No, she'd have her Zakes any day of the week.

* * *

Amanda listened to Zakes snore and knew he was really soused. Did he understand how annoying the snoring was? She would never get any sleep.

She forced her thoughts back to Zingisa once more. Her son, at nine years old, was fast growing into manhood and his father needed to shape up. The boy needed a better role model than a father who drank and drove and then spent all night snoring like a chain saw. Her annoyance with Zakes grew. But so did her annoyance with herself. Why did she pick on Zakes so much?

For a long while, she stayed in that dreamy-angry-sad zone, not fully awake, not yet asleep.

In that somnolent state, neither asleep nor fully awake, Amanda found herself transported back to Hamilton's house, to the beginning of the end of it all.

12 September 2002
MILNERTON

The stench hits you, grows with each step you take towards the bedroom, now the sickroom. The door is closed, but the odour is insistent. It is everywhere. Disinfectant, air freshener, Indian sticks, aromatic candles – nothing seems to make a difference, the suffocating smell reigns supreme.

The door is in fact slightly ajar. Like a thief, Amanda approaches it and carefully lays her trembling hand on the hard metal knob. She came at this hour, this day, knowing full well that Mamkwayi would be alone with her.

She tiptoes in. Then stops dead.

Dear God! There she lies, shrunken and skeletal. Only the head is still the same size – now seeming huge, disproportionate to the rest of her. And in that huge head, her eyes are two deeply sunken coals.

Remember how startled you were at your birthday lunch at the Town House, only a few weeks ago? Amanda thinks. Well, look at her now.

Bone.

Nothing but bone. That is what she has become.

But the voice is as strong as ever. "Sithandwa!" she croons as Amanda's hand takes hers.

Amanda bends and hugs the frail frame as best she can. She hugs her, praying all the while that the fear gnawing at her heart, at her soul, does not transmit itself through her arms and hands. Of all things, she doesn't want Beauty to know how scared she is. She doesn't want her to feel or sense the cold terror gripping her heart. Beauty must be scared enough as it is; she doesn't need anybody to add to that fear.

"How are you doing, sweetheart?"

Does she hear the tremor in my voice? Amanda wonders. The voice she strives so hard to make confident?

To allay her own fears, she goes for a stray lock lying on the pillow. She brushes it into harmony, tucks it back into the pattern. Gently. Gently. Thank God, her locks are as lustrous as ever. Beauty always loved her hair. God, please, leave her that. Leave her something. Don't take everything away from her. Please, let her keep her hair until . . . until . . .

"All the better for seeing . . ." Beauty stops abruptly, even though she has not yet run out of breath.

During the brief pause, Mamkwayi shakes her head, slowly, sadly.

The stumble shoots an arrow straight into Amanda's heart, reminding her (as though she could forget) that Beauty can no longer see anything. Those bright eyes burn in vain.

". . . now that you've come!" Beauty continues.

"She will not eat," Mamkwayi's voice penetrates the fog that envelops Amanda.

Amanda looks up. Sorrow and disbelief are married in the mother's eyes, each battling for supremacy. Like the other FFF mothers, Mamkwayi worked all her life as a domestic, stopping only when Beauty started teaching. Her brother, Mpumelelo, is more sponge than support to his parents. But Beauty supported her parents as all good African children do.

And now Beauty lies here, on what is most probably her deathbed. Dear God! When and how did Mamkwayi turn over this cruel new page where it is written that parents shall bury their children?

"Will not eat?" Amanda echoes stupidly. She doesn't know what to say. She doesn't want to say too many words — some will come out wrong. The less she says, the better.

"When she eats . . . anything," says the mother, her voice heavy with despair, "it runs straight through her."

A tear rolls out of Beauty's eye. She is lying on her side, and the un-checked tear falls over the bridge of her nose and down into the other eye. Then, out it spills again, and sinks into the soft, pale yellow pillow cradling her gaunt cheek.

"I have to change her," says Mamkwayi.

This is a major operation, as Amanda knows from previous visits. Covered in angry-looking, oozing sores, Beauty cries out and curses when touched anywhere except on her face, hands or neck. Everywhere else is a no-go zone.

"Let me help you!"

Mamkwayi nods and bustles out to get a few things she will need for the task at hand.

Soon they are busy.

When they are done and Beauty seems comfortable, Mamkwayi hastily prepares to go out. Today is Thursday. She is a member of the Mothers' Union and hasn't been able to attend meetings for weeks, a lack she feels sorely. Thanks to Amanda, today she can go.

* * *

"Eish, girl!" says Doris, head waving from side to side in an exaggerated gesture of admiration. "You look cheerful enough, now give us something to cheer us up."

Amanda raises one weary brow. "What do you suggest I wear on these visits?" she asks. "Black?"

Dressed in a pink jacket that picks up the pink in her tight floral pants, she ought indeed to be the picture of joie de vivre. She forces a smile onto her face and begins. The faces around her immediately grow sombre, but Amanda presses on. The listeners wouldn't want her to stop.

Cordelia, Edith and Doris listen as Amanda recounts the details of yet another visit. She tells; they listen. If only they could have been there themselves. So many of the details are lost in the telling. The FFF listen and try to read between the lines. But sometimes the lines are jagged, and the betweens all messed up. At other times the lines, quicksilver slippery, disappear before the FFF can read between them. But they listen all the same. And whatever they read into what Amanda relays, they cling to the unwavering belief that Beauty will mend. She will get better.

"Is she taking the right medication?" Doris asks.

"Who knows?" Amanda retorts, her eyes dead.

Both Mamkwayi and Hamilton are keeping mum on exactly what Beauty's illness is, never mind details about medication. The question Doris now asks reminds Amanda of her failure, her betrayal of her friend's wish. Even though Beauty has asked her to tell them her secret, she can't. She doesn't understand why, but she just can't. Just as there are things about her, Amanda, that she keeps to herself – for no reason at all. Now, she just can't find the right words or the right time, the moment, to say what Beauty has asked her to say. The FFF have to know, must know, but

60

when and what does she tell them, and how? Right now she is too angry. She will tell them, just not now. She will tell them because, after all, Beauty wants her to tell them. This is not her secret, not her shame. Besides, how can she answer them when she hasn't asked Beauty about medication or treatment? Beauty hadn't gone beyond the fatal word, and Amanda hadn't had the presence of mind to ask any questions – she was shocked numb.

"We should ask him," says Doris. "We owe it to Beauty to make sure she is getting the treatment she needs and deserves."

"Yes, of course," Edith says.

Cordelia bunches her brows. "Ask him? Why? Why would he tell us? He didn't even tell us Beauty was in hospital."

"Beauty needs our help," Amanda says, her voice small, as though she were talking to herself.

* * *

Zakes is watching television in the living room when Amanda walks in. Up till that moment she has held her feelings in, but now that she is finally back home, all that bottled-up gemors comes flying out.

Hearing the door open, Zakes had swung around and waved carelessly, but the silence startles him into taking another look. And that is when he is surprised by the flood gushing down his wife's cheeks.

"What's wrong?" He gets up so abruptly that the stool on which he is sitting overturns.

"Beauty!" Her voice is that of a scared six-year-old.

"No! Dead?"

Amanda's face crumples. "Don't say that!" she screams at Zakes, clinging to him desperately as she sobs.

* * *

Amanda is still in bed when the phone rings, very early the next morning. She glances at the bedside clock. It glows green in the pitch-dark of a wintry pre-dawn: 4:38.

"Hello?" she says.

"Beauty passed away at two-thirty." Mamkwayi's voice is flat, exhausted.

That long ago? How come she had no inkling? She should have had some premonition . . . should have known Beauty was dying . . . is dead. Her mind whirling, Amanda cannot find the words she needs to say.

"She just stopped breathing . . . just stopped . . . breathing . . ." The mother's voice catches.

"I'm sorry." It is all Amanda can force out. She tries harder: "I will let the others know. And we'll be over, as soon as . . ."

A long, howling silence follows. There are no goodbyes, just the hollow sound of the phone receiver going down gently on both sides.

Zakes, also awakened by the screech of the phone, has followed the one side of the conversation and gathered the rest. For a while, they sit on the bed, feet on the floor, and silently hold hands until Amanda has gathered herself enough to do what must be done.

* * *

Amanda calls Edith first.

"She is gone."

But Edith is half asleep. "Who is this?"

Amanda starts sobbing.

"Amanda?"

"Ye-ess!" Amanda chokes.

Sudden illumination floods Edith. She knows. "Beauty? It's Beauty, isn't it?" She doesn't need Amanda to tell her any more. Her sobs say it all.

"Have you told the others?"

Amanda shakes her head, forgetting that Edith cannot see the answer she gives, but her friend reads the silence correctly.

"All right then," says Edith. "I'll call them, then I'll come back to you."

Somehow, Edith has understood all that Amanda needs of her.

*   *   *

For all four remaining members of the FFF, sleep is out of the question after that. And, at the crack of dawn, the dishevelled, red-eyed young women, their heads covered and shawls over their shoulders, present themselves before Beauty's mother.

10 | *Sunday, 29 September 2002*
8 MNGA STREET, MALUNGA PARK

Ukusezw' amanzi – being made to drink water – is the ceremony held the day after a funeral. Its purpose is to comfort the bereaved, and it is simple and usually short.

Cordelia had called Edith the previous night and asked for a lift into Gugulethu. Edith had guessed from her curt tone that Cordelia was annoyed by whatever arrangement she and her husband had made about the car. She was surprised. What had made Cordelia give in to Vuyo? She was so strong. Certainly, she didn't dance to her husband's tune as did most wives Edith knew. Not Cordelia.

After picking up Cordelia, Edith drove to NY 74, as arranged, to collect Amanda and Doris. From there they made their way over to Malunga Park.

In German-print dresses – they had left the clothes they would be wearing to the Sonti funeral in the boot of Edith's car – they were shown to the room where Mamkwayi sat with a few women who were her age-mates or older.

Mamkwayi looked tired, but she seemed to have accepted what she could not change. She welcomed the FFF with a smile and, briefly, they talked of this and that, carefully avoiding what was uppermost in all their minds.

In the midst of the conversation, Mamkwayi suddenly sighed, stopping all talk. "Bantwana bam!" she said, taking advantage of the quiet she'd so cleverly engineered. "God has visited a hardship on us!" She shook her head. "But when I think of our friends, the Sontis, I wonder how they can bear a pain so huge. One child about to be buried and another on his deathbed!"

It was generally agreed that the other young man, twin to the one they were burying that day, didn't have long to live.

They didn't stay long with Mamkwayi. As young women, the FFF were expected to help with preparing the meal that would follow the ceremony. They knew that the younger women – family and neighbours – would have already started to prepare the meal and they were keen to help with the day's chores. It was one of the last things they'd ever be able to do for Beauty.

The young men of the family had just finished slaughtering a sheep when the FFF arrived. Now, Cordelia and Doris went out to the two makotis kneeling over huge plastic basins in the back yard. These were Nomvo and Sange, whose new blue German-print dresses announced their newlywed status. The old-fashioned way they were cleaning the innards marked them as novices. Cordelia quickly took over. She dragged over the garden hose and thrust it into the opening of each intestine, letting the water do the flushing. What would have taken each woman a full hour or more was done in seconds.

The same could not be said of the work Edith and Amanda had chosen. They'd joined the vegetable-chopping crew. In the kitchen, all you could hear was the sound of a small army of knives. Chop-chop. Chop-chop. It seemed to go on forever. Chop-chop-chop. Chop-chop-chop.

While waiting for the rest of the food, the men put some of the meat, set aside for that purpose, directly on the open fire to roast and eat.

While the cooking was under way, the eldest of the men, Tatomkhul' uXolo, took some of what the women had cleaned out of the innards before Cordelia had interfered with the time-honoured process, put it into a beaker, mixed it with bile from the slaughtered beast, and then added a little water to thin the mixture to a thick but drinkable consistency.

The old man then called over the family, clan relatives and friends. The small group made its way to the spot in the yard where the slaughtering had taken place, forming a solemn circle. Tatomkhul' uXolo said a few words to the Ancestors before leading everyone to the gate, where each in turn was handed the beaker containing the bitter mixture.

"Take a sip," said the old man. "Swirl it around in your mouth, and then step just outside the gate and spit it out."

This formality over, the food that had been cooking was ready. Plates flew from hand to eager hand, people ate and conversed, and the ceremony was over. Done. In two hours flat!

Only those washing Beauty's clothes were still at it. After a short break for the meal, clad in bicycle shorts and sports bras, they went back to work. Once washed, all her clothes would be divided among relatives and friends. Each of the FFF would get an item or two.

Hastily, the FFF fetched the clothes they'd left in the car and changed into appropriate funeral gear. Once ready, they accompanied Beauty's parents to the home of the Sonti family, bracing themselves for a second funeral in two days.

* * *

NY 1, north of NY 108, is in Section 3 of Gugulethu, a short distance from Malunga Park. By the time the party arrived at the Sonti home, clearly marked by the red-, white-and-green tent outside, the service was already under way. As Beauty's parents made their way inside the house, the FFF proceeded directly to the tent.

Several lay preachers presided. This suggested that the deceased had not attended church regularly. These days many ministers, overburdened by the weight of death on all sides, only conduct funerals for staunch members of their congregations. However, even taking this into account, the funeral service was much abbreviated and very subdued, due to the grave illness of the twin of the young man who was being buried.

Thereafter, the family led the procession to the graveyard. The Sontis lived not far from the NY 5 cemetery, but the service at the grave was also brief – threatened, as it was, by rain.

As the procession returning from the cemetery neared the Sonti home, a commotion broke out around the car bearing the chief mourners. They're overwhelmed, thought Amanda, it was no doubt all too much for the elderly parents to take in.

The FFF did not stay after the hand-washing ceremony. As Mamkwayi and Tata Mtini were not expected to stay under the circumstances, the FFF escorted them home, and then went on their way.

* * *

"Why do I have this feeling of déjà vu?" Doris said under her breath as the car rounded the corner of NY 68 and nosed its way into NY 74.

Just as had happened the day before, Thandi and her cronies were linger-ing in the street outside Amanda's gate. The FFF immediately recognised Moses and Zolile. Pleasantries were exchanged, one thing led to another, and before she knew what she was doing, Amanda, not wanting to appear unneighbourly, had invited Thandi and her friends inside.

"Thandi says you're coming from the funeral of the teacher who died of Aids," said Gabula, one of the four men in Thandi's group, before they had even taken their seats.

Amanda groaned inwardly. This threatened to be as nasty as the en-counter the previous afternoon. What had possessed her to invite these people inside?

"Two teachers buried in two days, and now another one dead," Thandi said. "Ziyaphel' iititshala! The teachers are disappearing!"

"Even the government says that," Samantha, another of Thandi's friends, said rather brightly. "Have you heard what happened today, at the Sontis?"

Exasperated, Amanda shook her head. Gossip to Samantha was like a hot potato in a child's hand. She'd sooner die than keep it to herself.

"You haven't heard what happened to the Sontis?" Moses asked. "The other twin has died too."

"No!" Edith snapped uncharacteristically.

"Yes!"

"No," said Amanda, her voice low. "Today, *one* of the twins was buried. The other twin is also ill. *Very* ill . . ."

Thandi saw the disbelief in her eyes. "The funeral party was on its way back from the graveyard when news reached them that the other twin had also passed away," she explained.

Amanda remembered the commotion that had broken out as the funeral procession had neared the Sonti home. Suddenly, the disturbance around the chief mourners' car now made awful sense.

Thandi clucked her tongue. "They aren't even going to take the tent down," she said. "The funeral will be on Wednesday."

A stunned silence followed as the FFF tried to come to grips with the news.

"Was his girlfriend there?" Moses asked. "And does she look like she's got it too?"

"You can't tell by looking!" Doris cried.

"Those girls, the girlfriends of the twin brothers," said Moses, shaking his head sadly, "they will give this Aids thing to other brothers, unless they also die!"

Cordelia had heard enough. "Hey, broer!" she shouted. "You are just assuming the twins were infected by their girlfriends."

"Everybody knows that is how men get Aids," said Gabula.

"But if a man sleeps with more than one partner, how can he be absolutely sure his girlfriend is the one who gave the disease to him?" Cordelia asked.

The men were silent.

"Personally," Cordelia continued, "I am more concerned for their girlfriends. I hope those women protected themselves."

"You mean, used condoms?" asked Moses scornfully.

"Sure!" Cordelia replied.

"Wow!" Gabula scoffed.

"Wow, what?" Cordelia raised her brows at him.

Both men gave disparaging laughs. Thandi and her female friends twittered self-consciously.

"Jaa!" roared Moses. "The brothers say using a condom is like eating sweets with the wrapper on!"

"And what do *you* say?" asked Cordelia.

"Me?" Surprised, he scratched his short-cropped head nervously.

"Yes, you," Cordelia said, stabbing at his chest with her index finger.

Leaning back, he said, "Serious?"

"As the back of your pyjamas!"

"Hey, suster," Gabula huffed, "you're taking this whole thing personal-like!"

"Life *is* very personal, if you ask me. And we're talking about life here, and death. Men who refuse to use condoms kill women!"

"No, my suster," Moses was adamant, "you can't blame men when it is these women who throw themselves at the men."

Cordelia glared at them, disgust in her eyes. "Yes," she said, "I can just see these women. They unzip the helpless men, pull out their diddles and thrust them into their hot kukus!"

"Suster," Moses objected, "not all black men are promiscuous – nga-mahenyu!"

"And what about the millions who *do* cheat on their wives, huh?" Cordelia asked.

"No, man!" Gabula grumbled, turning to Moses. "This suster, she is un-reasonable, mfowethu!"

"And Africans dying like flies from Aids is reasonable?"

"Aids is not a black thing," countered Moses.

"Uh-huh? How many white Aids orphans have you counted lately?" Cordelia shot back. "African mothers, faithfully married women, are killed by men who will not stop sleeping around!"

70

"You hate black men, don't you?" Gabula asked, nodding vehemently.

Cordelia continued as though he had not spoken. But her words showed that she had not only heard the question, but was ready, willing and eager to answer it.

"I hate my black brothers, you say? You're damn right I do!"

At this, all present started, including the FFF.

"Only a fool goes to bed with the enemy – an armed enemy, at that. What do you think the black man's penis is? I'll tell you what it is. It is a deadly weapon!"

She paused and shook her head. They were all so young. Every person in that room was under the age of forty. And unless something drastic happened to change their attitude, they were all walking corpses.

"We should *all* despise these men," she continued, almost shouting now. "Hate them! Hate them! Hate them!"

Abruptly, the four men stood up. They were leaving, they said. They were going to go and have a great time at Pepsi's Shebeen. They didn't have to listen to this kak.

* * *

"God!" Amanda said with feeling as she closed the door and, for a second, leaned against it.

Doris looked around at the others with an inquiring look on her face.

"What is it, why are you looking at us like that?" Amanda asked.

"We're just going to accept what they told us?" Doris asked, nodding towards the door.

"What they've told us . . .?" again Amanda asked.

"That the other Sonti twin has died."

After a brief discussion, Amanda phoned the Mtinis and discovered that, bitter though it may be, the truth does not change at our convenience.

"Mntwana wam," Mamkwayi had said as soon as she'd heard Amanda's voice on the phone. "God is truly judging us!"

They'd missed hearing about the second twin's death only because they hadn't stayed after washing their hands.

A brief silence followed as each woman digested the news. Then Doris said, "You know, those men may be ignorant, but they are right about one thing. Aids is not a black disease."

"Of course Aids is not a black disease!" cried Amanda. "But Doris, let's be honest, in this country, more black people are killed by Aids than any other group, than all the other groups put together!"

"Well," said Doris, "there *are* more black people in this country than any other group, you know that."

Since the departure of Thandi and her crew, Cordelia had not said a word, but Doris's comment roused her.

Shaking her head sadly, she said, "And Aids will continue to kill us as long as we refuse to take responsibility for our actions. See how many of that 'more' remain then!" She paused and closed her eyes.

Cordelia's words had pierced a chink in the armour Amanda wore. Why hadn't she carried out Beauty's wishes? What was she hiding? Surely she wasn't protecting Beauty? Protecting her from what? Then was she, Amanda, ashamed that her closest friend had had Aids?

Seeing the troubled look that had stolen over her face, and guessing at its origin, the others let Amanda be. A heavy and thoughtful silence fell.

At last, Amanda sighed. "I have a confession to make," she said, rubbing her forehead wearily.

All three looked up, keen interest on their faces.

"Before she died, Beauty asked me to tell you something."

You could have heard the proverbial pin drop.

"Remember the day Hamilton came in unexpectedly, so she didn't have a chance to finish what she was saying?"

Of course they did.

"Well," Amanda went on, "I don't know why . . . I just found myself incapable of telling you this. I think . . ."

Amanda started, stopped and started again. But, eventually, out came the story of her last visit to Beauty . . . the last visit while her friend had still been able to talk.

* * *

Mamkwayi has left her in attendance. It is a Thursday afternoon and the elderly woman has seized the opportunity to attend the Mothers' Union meeting. This group of prayerful women is a great source of strength to her. Therefore, in her uniform – black skirt, low-heeled black shoes, purple blouse and purple cape, with Bible and hymn book in bag – she kisses Beauty, bids Amanda goodbye, and leaves.

No sooner do they hear the front door close than Beauty stirs. "Sithandwa," she says, a smile tugging at the corners of her mouth.

"Yes, me dear?" Amanda teases.

"Hamilton stopped me, the other day. Remember?"

"I know."

"That can't happen today!" There is urgency in her voice.

Amanda takes one of Beauty's hands and gives it a firm squeeze.

From the answering squeeze, it is clear Beauty is intent on going on. Her voice emphatic, she speaks quickly, leaving Amanda not a moment to respond. "Promise me to live," she says. "Live to a ripe old age!"

Miraculously, there is suddenly no sign of the breathlessness Amanda so fears.

"Don't die a stupid death, like I am doing! Live!" she says. "Live till every hair on your head turns grey. Earn your wrinkles and, damn you, enjoy them! Enjoy every wrinkle and every grey hair on your head. Tell yourself you have survived! Sur-vived!" Her voice drops. "Live!" she says. "Don't die . . ."

Slowly, she moves her head from side to side.

"Don't die like . . . like . . . this . . ."

The low, hushed voice is but a whisper. Again, automatically almost, Amanda gives her friend's hand a gentle squeeze, amazed at the words from her mouth.

"And tell the others. Tell them what I say to you now. I have Aids," Beauty whispers. "Aids."

She closes her eyes and draws in a long, long breath, then she sighs and lets her body settle into the bed.

*　*　*

Amanda came to the end. Head bowed, she waited. She was apprehen-

74

sive, but she was also filled with relief that she had finally discharged her duty, had done right by her friend.

Around her there was absolute silence as the three women mulled over what Amanda had revealed to them. She looked up at the faces of her FFF sisters, looked at each one, pleadingly, one by one. But each face was bathed in wonderment. All seemed in awe of what Amanda's revelation spelled: Beauty had loved them to the very last. What a gift!

Finally, Edith broke the silence. "This is God in action," she said quietly. "The Almighty uses us, plain ordinary people, when we are willing to be instruments of His will. In the midst of her own suffering, Beauty found the courage to speak up so as to save us from a similar fate. And that," she added, "is grace!"

Her face sombre, Doris said, "I can't say you do not speak the truth, my friend. And now that I think back the signs were there, but we ignored them, I suppose . . ."

"Or hoped they would disappear," confirmed Cordelia. "Just when we thought we saw something that said our friend might be unwell, the signs would disappear completely and . . ."

". . . she would look okay again," Edith finished the sentence for her. She threw an imploring eye at Doris and Amanda. "Remember?"

"She looked picture-perfect at your discussion group, Doris," said Amanda. "Didn't she?" she added, as though to reassure herself.

"But do you remember how upset she got about that line in the poem: 'death is the mother of beauty'?" Cordelia said. "We all thought she was being irrational. Now I wonder . . ." she left the thought unfinished.

Edith sighed. "Poor woman!" she said, cupping her chin in both hands. "But how could she get Aids, married and faithful and all?"

"Hello?" Cordelia said. "We all know Hamilton likes yanga-yangas!"

"But he looks fine," Edith said. "Did you see how well he looked at the funeral?"

"The brother's sure as hell getting some help, somewhere," Cordelia growled. "But let's see how long that lasts. Unless he stops messing around, he'll just keep on getting himself re-infected – and all the ARVs in the world won't help him in the end."

The women exchanged sad, knowing glances.

"The leopard never changes his spots," Edith said quietly.

Doris had heard enough. "Friends," she said, "all that is past tense now. Let's get on with our business."

Then, like children learning to walk, taking the first tentative steps, the four women began to discuss the issue Amanda had laid before them: how to live to old age . . . how to save their own lives.

"Where do you think we should start?" Doris wondered out loud.

"Amanda should tell us that," said Cordelia. "She's had more time to think about it."

Amanda bit her tongue. She understood this was Cordelia's way of showing her how stupid she had been, keeping quiet for so long. But she also knew that Cordelia's anger would pass.

"How about we look at what killed her and make sure it doesn't kill us?" said Cordelia when Amanda remained silent. "That would be a good starting point, I think."

"No sex?" Doris asked.

"No sex without an Aids test!" Cordelia said.

"But what if Luvo refuses to get himself tested?" Edith asked.

"Then you insist that he uses a condom," Cordelia replied.

"But what if he refuses that, too?" Edith countered.

Doris jumped in. "Friend," she said, "we're talking about life and death here. This is what Beauty warned us of. This is what she wanted us always to remember."

"But what about 'be loyal'?" Edith asked.

"How are you going to monitor that?" Cordelia asked in turn. "One of my own brothers has thirteen children. Thirteen! From five or six different women. I lost count in the end. And this man is supposed to be happily married."

Cordelia's words stung Amanda. Cordelia could have been speaking of her own brothers – the younger two, that is, Mandla and Luntu. Last time she'd bothered to count, they had twenty-one children between the two of them – and only three of those with their wives. More and more, Amanda was not only disappointed in her brothers, but disgusted and angry with them. Only bhuti PP didn't have "outside children" or "grass children", as they were sometimes called. But PP, as Penrose Phaphama was popularly known, was a special case. He had married his childhood sweetheart, Nolusapho, and God had blessed the two with three drop-dead gorgeous daughters. While another man would have insisted that his wife go on having baby after baby because he wanted a son, PP had put a stop to all of that after Sethu's birth. He wasn't putting Nolusapho through all that pain again, not for anything. And because it was easier for a man, he had a vasectomy. It was sometimes difficult for Amanda to believe that Mandla and Luntu were related to PP.

"You're all supposedly in monogamous relationships," Cordelia continued, looking at each one of her friends. "But *are* they really monogamous, or are you being lied to?" She made a face as if she'd swallowed a live reptile. "I *know* Vuyo is not loyal to me."

"I suppose that is what killed our friend!" Edith said.

"Suppose, my foot!" Cordelia said bitterly. "We all know it's the gospel truth. Beauty would be here today if Hamilton had been loyal to her."

Amanda agreed wholeheartedly. "This, my friends, is the choice before us," she said in a voice hoarse with feeling, and the others knew, at that moment, that Beauty was in the room with them.

"So what does all this mean for us . . . for each one of us?" Doris asked.

"Beauty wouldn't want us to be sad, she would want us to fight to live, to fight for our lives," Amanda said. "And I think that together, supporting each other, we can make it."

11

Homeward bound, Amanda felt buoyant. She was relieved she had finally got the whole thing off her chest. She was just sad it had taken her all this time to get round to doing it. She wouldn't make the same mistake with Zakes, she vowed, anticipating his understanding. Surely he would be receptive?

However, when she got home, Zakes's lovey-dovey jokes and grabby-feely fingers told Amanda loud and clear exactly what he wanted. She would have to do a lot of explaining, for Zakes could be both persuasive and insistent when it came to his manly needs. Well, she'd just do what she had to do. No test, no unprotected sex. Take it or leave it!

Amanda went to have a shower, taking her time over it, and returned to the bedroom to find her husband on her side of the bed. Apparently, Zakes was fixed on his plans for the night.

"Please move over to your side," she asked him.

"Mandy, please, sweetheart."

"No, Zakes. Not tonight. I can't."

"Please, sweet thing, let me sip some of that honey on the rock."

"Zakes, no," she hissed. "I said no!"

But her refusal only seemed to fuel his desire. "Please, Mama Ama," he groaned, seizing her hand and drawing it to his ramrod-stiff member.

"No!" Amanda shrieked, snatching away her hand as though what throbbed beneath it were a live snake.

"Why?" barked Zakes, waking up to the reality that his wife was in no mood for sex.

"What do you mean, 'why'?" Amanda barked right back, more resolved to tackle the issue than she'd ever been before. "Zakes, I think we need to talk about getting an Aids test."

"Wha-aat?" Zakes asked, staring at her as though she had just fallen through the ceiling.

Amanda stared right back, but said absolutely nothing. She reckoned he'd heard her pretty well.

"What's this about a test, huh?"

"I said we should think about taking an HIV test."

"Because . . .?" he said, quietly, so that she knew he was truly angry. When Zakes was annoyed, he yelled. When he grew quiet, he was seething.

"Because it's the only way to know where we stand," she said, pausing to look at his incredulous face. "Everybody says testing and using condoms saves lives."

Zakes jumped off the bed. "Are you accusing me of something?" he growled. "What? Out with it! Or are you fooling around?"

Amanda nearly burst out laughing. The spectacle of a furious Zakes – naked as the day he was born, his manhood all shrivelled up, dangling between his thighs – was just too ludicrous for words.

Finally, she got herself under control. "Nothing!" she said, making sure her voice was reasonable and patient. "Zakes, this is neither accusation nor admission of unfaithfulness. But our lives are at stake here. Faithfully married women are dying of Aids. I just think it is the –"

"Is that right?" Zakes flopped back onto the bed, covering his nakedness with the sheet. "Just because Hamilton is a womaniser, suddenly we are all dogs?"

"No, Zakes," she said. "But these days love and loving is about protecting those you love. It is about caring enough for the one you love to –"

"That so?"

"Yes . . . to make sure they are safe, Zakes. It is about taking responsibility for one's health and the safety of one's partner," she said earnestly, taking his hand in hers. "It is about the two of us making sure that we will live long enough to see Zingisa's children."

"So, I must take an Aids test? But we're married, 'Manda!" whined Zakes, snatching his hand away.

"Then let's do the test. Is that too much to ask?"

They argued until Amanda realised it was pointless. They weren't getting anywhere. "It's late," she said and yawned. "I'll sleep in the spare room."

She didn't wait for a response. Fortunately, the bed in the spare room always had fresh linen, so she could crawl between the sheets right away.

Come morning, Zakes would be more reasonable. He usually was. By nature, he was not a bad man. Not really.

12 | *Wednesday, 2 October 2002*
NY 1, NO. 33, GUGULETHU

In general, funerals are sad affairs, but Lungile Sonti's funeral was far from sombre. While no one could say the air was jolly, there was something strange in the atmosphere – a feeling of suppressed excitement, of anticipation, almost.

Amanda, Edith and Cordelia (uncharacteristically camouflaged by huge sunglasses) arrived ten minutes before the hearse was expected – Doris was unable to attend as she was busy in court that day.

The place was packed. The Department of Education had given teachers leave to go to the funeral and there were teachers in droves, busloads of students, rugby players, sportspeople and more. Lunga's funeral, four days before, had been a well-attended, if subdued, affair. But the aberration of Lungile's death, and the circumstances surrounding it, had so startled the population of Gugulethu that people had come to hear and see for themselves what this family would say, how it was coping with so huge a tragedy. Even in these times of "the disease of the children", no one had ever heard of such an abomination, where on the day one child was buried another child had died. One woman was heard to say, "Kuphekwa enye ngomhluzi wenye! – One is cooked with the gravy of another!"

How could this family possibly cope?

* * *

Three girls and three boys lined up at the gate to the humble family home. Each held a basket of red ribbons, which they handed out as people walked in. And that was the first thing that struck the three women – the sea of red.

Every breast sported a red ribbon. The Sonti family was on a mission. United, they were not only openly declaring the cause of Lungile's death, they were seizing the chance to educate the community.

"I wish Doris were here," Edith whispered to the other two.

They nodded their agreement.

"Everybody should see this!" she continued.

Inside, another set of boys and girls handed out pamphlets on HIV and Aids, as well as other sexually transmitted diseases, along with the programmes.

The FFF were given their pamphlets and programmes and shown to their seats in a tent set aside for the teachers and sportspeople. Lungile had played wing for the Spring Roses, one of the local rugby teams.

The burial service was brief, to accommodate the speakers: four in all. The first spoke about Lungile's illness on behalf of the family. The next gentleman described Lungile's illustrious role in the formation and development of the rugby union in the Western Cape. He then conveyed that body's condolences to the Sonti family. The third speaker was a member of Vukani, a local NGO, who spoke of her ten-year journey of living with HIV. Looking at her, it was evident that there was no way of telling from a person's physical appearance whether or not they were infected – Nomtha Langa was a picture of radiant health. And what she said was instructive to anyone with ears to hear. She stressed that to test HIV positive was not a death sentence. "However," she went on, "I am faced every day with a series of choices, choices that could spell life or death not only for myself, but for others . . ."

According to the programme, the last speaker was a community leader. Mrs Mazwi had taught Lungile. In fact, she had taught many of the teachers present that day. Now retired, she was very involved in the affairs of the community and greatly respected for it.

"It gives me great joy to see so many of you here today," she began. "I am particularly happy to see the youth. For, my children, let us not beat about the bush, this is your funeral. This is your disease. This is your time of judgement. But it is also your challenge, your call to higher duty!"

She paused, and looked around at the young people who made up more than half of the assembly. So many, it brought a lump to her throat. They were walking corpses if nothing was done. Something had to be done soon. Something bold. Something real.

She took a deep breath, smiled confidingly, and continued, "I'm not going to ask a hard maths question. But hands up, all those who have no illegitimate children in their families."

A brief twitter rippled through the audience as, silently, Mrs Mazwi surveyed the results of her on-the-spot research.

"From where I am standing," she said, "there is not one hand I can see. Look around you. Look!"

She paused as people did as she said, heads turning this way and that.

"That is how it is going to be with Aids. Very soon, all our families will have at least one person infected with HIV. One, if we are lucky. What has happened to the Sonti family will happen to many others. The same way a family may have two or three or more daughters who become mothers before they are married, or sons who become fathers before they are married, so it will be with Aids. Our families will all be affected, in exactly that way!"

A hush fell as those present, some perhaps for the first time, contemplated the enormity of the catastrophe towards which they were hurtling headlong.

"However," Mrs Mazwi continued, "we are, fortunately, not doomed to die. Don't let sex kill you. Use condoms. Stay faithful. Test and test again. Testing gives you a tremendous advantage. The earlier you know you are sick, the sooner you can get medical help, the better your body is able to help you stay healthy. Therefore, early detection is the best medicine. Test, test and test again, I urge you all."

Mrs Mazwi raised a hand in salute, like the anti-apartheid leaders of old. "Let us fight back! Don't let the busy-tongued gossip stop you from testing! Don't let him stop you from getting the medicine you need! There is no stigma to fighting to stay alive. There is no stigma to illness. If you're ill, you're ill, not dirty! The stigma belongs to those who gossip!"

She had to stop, for the crowd was applauding tumultuously, stirred by her words. She paused to acknowledge the unity of feeling.

"In our homes," she went on when quiet was restored, "let us talk to the children about sex."

A murmur rose up again from the crowd. At once, she put up her hand to still the people. "Let me remind you, maAfrika amahle, this is something we as a people used to do. Isn't that something? That the so-called 'red person', the uneducated man, knew enough of nature to guide his child to sexual health? That the red woman, unsophisticated as she was, shepherded her daughter safely through puberty, a stage of life fraught with all sorts of danger? And yet we of today, believing ourselves educated and therefore better than our forebears, have abandoned their ways. My people, wake up! Vukani! Let us not abandon all the things that make us who we are. There may be a very good reason our Ancestors put those things in place."

She paused to catch her breath.

"And where is the government?" she asked, having recovered herself. "Where is the government, with our children dying? Listen to me. I am *not* standing here praying for apartheid to come back. I was as happy as the next person when that evil came to an end. But can you think what would have happened had this Aids pandemic come during apartheid? We would have cried 'Genocide!' had the apartheid government dragged its feet the way our democratically elected government is dragging its feet now – even as our people die in their thousands. What is more, the whole world would have supported us. The world would have condemned the genocide perpetrated by the apartheid government. So why are our lips sealed now? How is it that we let this government, *our* government, get away with mass murder? A genocide of the poor? Why are we allow-ing the government to squander the resources of our country on arms when the real war facing us demands antiretrovirals? We need knowledge and medicine to fight this war, not guns! And make no mistake, this is war! Are you going to stand and let Aids do what even apartheid could not do? Are you going to lose a war that can be so easily won? What will history say of us?"

Now, fist high in the air, she cried, "To all of us, I say: go and fight! And fight to win!"

At that, the FFF women looked at one another and smiled. Mrs Mazwi's words had struck a chord.

She waved to the crowd and took her seat to deafening applause.

* * *

"What did you think of the speech?"

Cordelia turned around to see Thandi's policeman friend regarding her with large mud-coloured eyes. He was wearing the same navy pants, white shirt and grey sports jacket he'd had on both times she'd seen him before, but hard as she tried, she could not remember the man's name. She smiled to hide her confusion. "Very good, wasn't it?"

"But she is painting the government black."

"It *is* black!" Cordelia said, still smiling.

The man didn't smile. "You know what I mean," he said.

"No, I don't!" Cordelia replied. "Are you saying we can't criticise the government?"

He drew himself up to his full height, cleared his throat and harrumphed his disapproval.

Irritated, Cordelia said, "Criticising the government is the very essence of democracy!"

"Washing our dirty linen in public?"

"No, helping our nation forward!"

"How are you helping when you criticise?" he shouted, causing a few faces with raised eyebrows to turn their way.

Cordelia stood her ground. "Our government can only benefit from criticism by its people. It is a government of the people and so, in fact, it should welcome hearing from those people . . ."

Just then Amanda, who had stepped away to say a few words to the Sontis, returned and Cordelia, breathing a sigh of relief, used the opportunity to make her escape.

* * *

What had she been thinking? Doris asked herself. She needed her head read. A young woman alone in a white four-by-four, waiting opposite a house known to be uninhabited. And at night. In the middle of Gugulethu. Was she looking for trouble or what? And where on earth were her friends?

Because they were teachers, Amanda, Cordelia and Edith had been given the day off to go to Lungile's funeral. Doris had had a hard day in court and waiting outside Amanda's township home for what seemed like a year had done nothing to improve her temper. "I hate sitting in the car in Gugulethu," she grumbled, scrambling out of the vehicle even before the first FFF car had come to a stop.

"Girl," said Cordelia, as she climbed out of her car, "you should have heard Mrs Mazwi at the funeral. Some of the teachers were asking for a copy of her speech afterwards."

"What did she say?" Doris asked Cordelia. "And what's with the sunglasses? It's evening!"

"It is up to each individual to fight the battle against Aids," Cordelia said, ignoring Doris's second question.

"She said much more," insisted Amanda as she opened the door to her home. "Her exact words were: 'Before long, there will not be one family left untouched by Aids. Not one!'"

"What a bleak forecast," Doris said as Cordelia brushed past her.

"Come on in, Edith!" Amanda called out, holding the door open.

Edith was getting out of the car, slowly, her movements listless.

Once they were all inside, the conversation quickly turned to more personal matters, as the four friends reported back on their attempts to seize Beauty's gift.

"How have things been for *you*?" Doris asked, turning to Amanda.

"Zakes and I have started our own little cold war!" Amanda told her. "He's not interested in testing. He says we're married."

At this, Edith burst into tears. And out came her story. Luvo wasn't speaking to her. He had accused her of disloyalty.

"He asked me what kind of a wife involves outsiders in her marriage," she sobbed.

"Outsiders?" Doris asked.

"My friends," replied Edith, nodding toward Doris and the other two. "You."

"How did we get involved in your marriage?" Doris asked.

Edith slowly shook her head. "It's enough that we *talked* about condoms!"

As Doris moved her chair closer to Edith, and drew her friend into an embrace, Cordelia slowly, deliberately, took off her glasses. Her left eye was swollen shut. "Well, you can see how *my* life has been going," she said, her voice trembling. "Vuyo has left me, he's moved out."

Things between the two had been rough for some time, but no one expected this. Both Cordelia and Vuyo were stubborn, but they were conscientious parents, dedicated to their children. Cordelia complained a lot about Vuyo, but she always praised him for nurturing their children – Vuyiswa and Vuyisile, twelve and ten, respectively.

"After our discussion," Cordelia continued, "I wouldn't entertain him without the use of a condom. So, he went and found himself what he calls 'a one-night thing'."

"But you knew Vuyo wasn't faithful," said Doris. "You told us so yourself."

"Yes, I did," replied Cordelia calmly, "but this time he admitted it openly. When I told him I was going to do the same, he threatened to kill me." Remembering the scene that had followed her threat, she closed her eyes for a moment. "No one has the right to expose another to Aids," she continued. "So, as far as I am concerned, Vuyo can go to hell! It's all over between us."

"What is the matter with these men?" Doris asked.

"They've had it too good, too long," Cordelia snapped.

"Amen to that!" said Edith, drying her tears.

"These men are all flour from the same Bokomo bag!" Amanda concluded.

In silence, the FFF regarded one another, each with her thoughts.

"I have a plan," Amanda said finally.

"All ears, girlfriend," said Cordelia.

"Why don't I cut keys to this house and let each one of you have a set?"

"Give us keys to your house?" asked Edith, eyes wide with hesitant hope.

"I hope to heaven none of you ever really need them," Amanda answered.

She got up and went to the door. A group of girls were skipping rope across the street. She called one of them to send her on an errand to the hardware store at the NY 50 shopping centre. "Tell him to make us four of each, please," she told the girl, handing over her keys and giving her a hundred-rand note.

While they waited for their keys, Doris told the group that she had persuaded Selby to join her in attending the premarital counselling classes her church offered.

"But will a course make him agree to going for testing?" Amanda asked.

Doris confessed that Selby had not exactly agreed to get himself tested. It just happened that he had to do it anyway.

"Because we're applying for a bond," she explained to her friends, "we both have to get tested. The bank strongly recommended that we get life insurance, and of course you can't get cover without being tested first."

Cordelia thought about what Doris had just told them. "That's the only way anyone will ever get Africans to go for testing. They'll never do it voluntarily," she said, remembering Mrs Mazwi's words.

For a while, they were quiet, thinking of what had just been said. Regardless of who did or did not want to know their status, the banks wanted to make sure they were lending their money to people who'd be around for a while – alive and able to pay them back. So Doris and Selby were going for the test the following week, no ifs, buts or maybes. No argument. The bank had decreed.

"Saved by the bank, then?" Cordelia said at last, lifting her eyes to Doris.

Doris nodded. "Yes, you could say that, but I think Sel would've agreed to go test anyway."

Edith produced a sad little smile. "Aren't you the lucky fish?"

Just then the girl Amanda had sent to the shopping centre returned. She had the keys in a crumpled plastic bag.

Amanda took the bag and handed her a five-rand coin from the change. "Go get yourself a vetkoek and a frikkie," she told her.

A huge smile on her face, the girl scampered away.

Amanda turned back to her FFF sisters. "Don't say I never do anything for you, now, hear me?" she said as she began to hand out the keys.

"The keys to *our* Gugs home, Amanda," Doris said, beaming.

Amanda smiled. "You're welcome, my friends."

"But why four?" Edith asked, taking her set of keys.

"Four?"

"Yes, Amanda," said Doris, also realising the mistake Amanda had made.

"I . . . I forgot, didn't I?" she said, the smile fading away and the corners of her mouth dipping southward.

Cordelia saw the sadness return to the group. "Thank you, friend of ours!" she said, before it took over. "It's good to know we have each other."

13 | *Saturday, 5 October 2002*
8 MNGA STREET, MALUNGA PARK

If a funeral is a busy and expensive affair, the spade-washing ceremony, a week after the funeral, is right there at its heels. Of course, there is no coffin, but anyone who has ever asked a few friends over for drinks or lunch knows how expensive such affairs can turn out to be. So, feeding the entire village always has been and always will be a financial hazard.

Wisely, Beauty's parents belonged to a burial society – they made monthly payments, and so had received a lump sum. This would see to everything: groceries, the hiring of pots, stoves, plates, cutlery, chairs and tables. The society would even be responsible for cleaning up after the event.

"Come!" called Mamkwayi, in her blue dress, leading the FFF to her bedroom, where they had spent so many hours in happier days – with her, and with Beauty. Mamkwayi, always available with laughter, advice, consolation and anything else they had needed, first as growing girls, and then as young women.

"My children," she said, spreading her hands, showing them where to perch themselves – on chair, stool and bed.

Politely but firmly, she turned down their offers of help. "Between all these makotis and the burial society people, there's no need for you to lift a finger."

The FFF seated themselves and waited, for they could all see that something burned Mamkwayi's chest.

But she started by remarking on the dark glasses Cordelia still wore.

"My eyes hurt," said Cordelia. And that was that.

Mamkwayi tut-tutted in sympathy. Then, still standing, she could contain herself no longer. Arms akimbo, nostrils flaring, her eyes bulging in amazed contempt, knowing that Beauty's friends would understand her outrage, she burst out: "Do you know that he's not coming? His parents are here. Sandile is here, of course. And his sister and brothers are here. But the king is not coming."

"Why?" asked Amanda. She didn't really care, part of her was actually relieved, but she was also angry with Hamilton for showing such disrespect to Beauty's parents. God, that's all these good people needed right now. How callous could the man be?

"He wanted the ceremony held at his place."

"When has such a thing ever happened?" Edith blurted out. "That the funeral service is held at one place, and then the spade-washing ceremony is held at another?"

"Hamilton has gone mad," Cordelia spat out. "Stark, raving mad."

Tiredly, Mamkwayi sank into a chair. "That is exactly what Beauty's father asked him," she said. "'How do we hold the funeral here, and then hold the spade-washing ceremony there?'"

"What did he say to that?" Doris asked.

"Oh, he said he only agreed to us holding the funeral service here because he wasn't thinking straight. He was still confused."

"Confused?"

"Yes, he had just lost his *darling* wife."

"Hamilton gets on my last nerve!" said Amanda in exasperation.

To everyone's surprise, Mamkwayi laughed. "He gets on Beauty's father's nerves too, I can tell you that. Hear this!"

She stood up tall, pushed her shoulders back and, scowling, made an annoyed Tata Mtini face. "Oh-oh, son-in-law!" she growled in a man's voice. "You think we should've waited a year before burying your wife? To give you time to get over your confusion? Eh?"

Mamkwayi mimicked Tata Mtini so well, the FFF fell into unrestrained laughter.

"My children," she said, "I couldn't agree more with Beauty's father. But the stubborn one only dances to the tune he himself sings – uxhents' ezombelela. Really, I don't know why we are surprised. He is a man who only ever listens to his own counsel. Even when his parents tried to reason with him, he wouldn't see his mistake."

"At least his family is here," Amanda said consolingly.

It *was* good that Beauty's in-laws had come. After all, Beauty was the mother of their grandson. Nothing could change that. The link between these two families hadn't ended when Beauty's life ended. Sandile was that link, and he needed all the nurturing both families could give him.

"Yes," said Mamkwayi, "his whole family is here. They came very early this morning. Let's thank God for that." She was quiet for a few moments. Then, shaking her head, she said, "His sister tells me they're all angry with him. They believe he shut Beauty's mouth towards the end."

"Did what?" Amanda burst out angrily.

"Yes, they say when I wasn't there, he sat by her bedside, day and night, and wouldn't let anyone near her." Again she shook her head. "They say that son-in-law somehow convinced my child that they should go to the grave with their secret." She paused. "Maybe he didn't want us to know which one of them gave this terrible disease to the other."

Just like that, as though she'd mentioned the nature of Beauty's illness to them previously, Mamkwayi had said what she'd never had the courage to utter before. Not to the FFF, at any rate.

"But we all know the answer to that," Cordelia burst out in surprise. "Beauty was an angel!"

Mamkwayi sighed, letting her shoulders droop. Then she straightened and smiled. "It does not matter now. My beautiful baby is at peace."

"When do we get to see Sandile?" Amanda asked, trying to change the subject.

No sooner had she asked than the boy was called in, and his FFF aunties handed him the small bag of goodies they'd brought for him.

Doris asked the khaki-clad, barefoot boy whether he had any of their telephone numbers.

"Yes, Auntie Dee," he said. "I have yours. And Auntie Ama's, Auntie Cord's and Auntie Eddy's!"

"Well, call us sometime," said Cordelia. "And come spend time with Vuyisile."

"And Vuyiswa?"

"Yes, of course."

He quickly peeked at the goodies, thanked his aunties, hugged them briefly, and left.

"The perfect gentleman," chortled Cordelia as Mamkwayi beamed with pride, her eyes fondly fixed on the receding figure.

At ten o'clock, they all went out into the yard, where the elders of the family were already gathered. By then the ceremony was well under way.

Symbolically, some umqombothi was poured over the spades, cleansing them. The spades used at Beauty's grave stood for everything associated with death and dying. They had been commandeered by death, but now they were restored and could once again be used for their usual, everyday tasks.

When they went back to the house, the FFF were directed to Beauty's bedroom. Two of the older women were sitting on grass mats on the floor with Mamkwayi. One of the makotis was standing demurely just inside the door. Hanging on rails along the walls were Beauty's suits. Such a splash of colour – red everywhere. Red or colours that went well with red, but never black. Beauty hardly ever wore black.

"She didn't like dark colours," observed Amanda.

"We feel you four, who were like her sisters, should choose first," a beaming Mamkwayi said, nodding in the direction of the FFF.

First, Amanda pointed to a three-piece suit, pants and skirt. Edith picked a long cashmere stole, Cordelia a headscarf and Doris a snazzy pair of shoes. All four FFF chose different things, but all of them had one thing in common – the colour red.

* * *

From Malunga Park, the FFF made their way to Amanda's township house – theirs now, for they all had keys to it. But the get-together could not last too long. Doris was meeting Selby that afternoon. "We have a three o'clock appointment with Father Mpambani," Doris said with shy pride – Father Mpambani was the rector at St Mary Magdalena Church.

Edith asked her when she and Selby were going for their HIV test.

"Next week."

"Good luck!" Beaming, Edith asked her about the classes she and Selby were attending with the priest.

"Oh, I love going to see Reverend Mpambani," said Doris. "He explains things so well. Makes you think things through more clearly. Even with this test thing, he'll find a way of weaving some biblical element into it, I'm sure. He's such fun. He's completely changed my view of priests."

She paused for a few seconds before adding, "Besides, he's marrying us . . . and advises counselling before marriage."

"Wish I'd gone for counselling before marriage," said Cordelia sardonically. "Perhaps I'd be singing a different tune today."

That cracked everybody up.

Doris stood up to leave, but before she parted from her FFF sisters they all joined in wishing her good luck with the test. A mere formality, really . . .

14

The single rose on the otherwise very masculine desk of Reverend Mpambani always intrigued Doris. Did his wife put it there? Or was it the home help? And why? She rather hoped it was his wife. Then she told herself she was being sentimental – after all, the couple had been married for more than twenty years. But in her heart of hearts, she still clung to the hope that Mrs Mpambani faithfully put a rose on her husband's desk each morning. Going into her own marriage, she desperately needed to see evidence of marriages that not only worked, but thrived. Especially with all the nonsense going on in her friends' marriages right now.

The man of God cast a shrewd glance at the young man sitting before him. Earnest, confident, handsome and prosperous-looking, yet without seeming preoccupied with his looks or good fortune. Reverend Mpambani gave an inward nod of approval.

"I think you're readier than most young couples I've had the honour of marrying in recent times," the priest said in his deep voice.

"Thank you, sir," replied Selby, smiling respectfully at the man of the cloth. Surreptitiously, he squeezed the butter-soft hand that lay in his, but Reverend Mpambani's next words brought him up sharp.

"Marriage is more difficult than most people like to think." The reverend paused, the barest hint of a smile at the corners of his mouth, his eyes wrinkling kindly. "Love, genuine love, is patient. It forgives all. It has no pride. It is selfless!"

Again he was silent, hands pressed together, the long fingers tapping against each other to some inner, unheard rhythm. Then he referred them to 1 Corinthians 13, verses 1 to 13, saying he believed that chapter explained the whole thing better and more clearly than anywhere else in the Bible.

"Read that passage for yourselves. Think about it, talk about it, and see how you can use it. Decide whether it offers any guidelines for the life you plan to live together and" – his shy smile broke out into a chuckle – "perhaps, the good Lord willing, with your little ones."

"Thank you, Father," Selby said shyly.

Doris found a warm smile breaking out over her face.

"That will be all for today, then," Reverend Mpambani said, taking a quick look at the watch on his wrist. He hoped he wasn't too late. Last rites were a tricky affair. Too early, and they upset the family – people wanted to cling to hope, even desperate hope. Too late, and they upset the family even more – people wanted to give their loved one a last chance to atone for sins they didn't really believe the dying had committed. To family members, their dear departing wore a mantle of sainthood, no matter what sort of life they had lived. The duties of a priest were far from easy.

* * *

A fine drizzle hung in the air as Doris and Selby dashed for the car –
Selby's white four-by-four. His mother lived in Mdantsane, near East
London, and a four-by-four was a necessity if you didn't want to leave
your engine somewhere along the roadside. The roads in Mdantsane had
potholes bigger than those in Harare.

"One minute more in that office, and we'd have been drenched!" laughed
Doris, buckling herself in.

"You wish!"

"I do?"

"Darling," he teased, "isn't that a little premature?"

"What?"

"I do!" Selby said, mimicking her. "You're supposed to say that at
the altar!"

He threw her a sly glance to see the effect of what he'd just said, but
Doris just shook her head and began humming.

He started the car and cruised away. Roiling dark clouds obscured the
sky, until only a glimpse here, a hint there, remained of the blue sky under
which they had walked into the rectory a little earlier.

Everyone was driving homewards from the city centre, and Selby had
the road to himself, except for the taxis, vying with each other at break-
neck speed for fares. In Rondebosch, they picked up takeaways for an
early supper at King's Wood, their favourite Chinese restaurant.

By now, the rain had become a storm. Selby parked as close as he could
to his flat, but the two-minute dash left them soaked to the skin.

They quickly changed into dry clothes, but first, Selby did one of his
favourite things: he wrapped Doris in a huge, fluffy towel and rubbed her
dry. Gently, tender as a mother drying a baby, he rubbed her from head to

toe, in and out of every fold and crevice of her body, the folds of her arms, her legs . . . even behind her ears. His wish had been granted after all.

They ate watching television. However, theirs was a hasty meal. They had something better to do. Much, much better! She was a violin, Selby a talented artist. And from her, out of that finely tuned instrument, the master brought the sweetest music with his bow.

Later, cradled in each other's arms, limbs entwined, they snoozed.

She was first to open her eyes. She closed them again and thought of how much she loved this man. Loved him with a love so fierce that at times it felt as though her heart would burst – a love too huge to be enclosed in even a heart as big as hers.

And, she knew it with absolute certainty, he loved her right back.

What could ever change that?

Then she remembered Beauty. She and Hamilton . . . had they ever felt this way about each other? If not, why would they have married each other? If they had, why had things turned out the way they did?

A cold fear gripped Doris. If this were not the most special, sacred feeling, then what was? And if it were, then how could it ever change?

She shook her head. Never! Their love for each other was real. It would never die. Neither would it tarnish or fade. If anything, with time, with children, with a growing understanding of each other, the love they had could only deepen. Become richer, sweeter. Oh, so much sweeter . . .

Sighing contentedly, she snuggled even closer as his arm drew her to his warm, sleep-softened body.

* * *

"Must you go home?" Selby groaned.

This was a running battle between the two of them. Her parents wanted a white wedding. They wanted to give their daughter away. Doris, one of seven children, had been the only one to finish high school. All her sisters had been teenage mothers. Her brothers had also had children before marriage. They all drank. They all had lousy jobs (those who actually had jobs). Doris's parents were so proud of her, and the last thing they wanted was to have her sneak out of their house and go and live with Selby before they were married. Yes, marriage negotiations had started. Yes, Selby could visit their daughter, and she could go and see him. This they understood. But that did not mean they were willing to give up their bragging rights to a white wedding.

"I told you I should have driven myself over . . ."

"What's the fuss? We're getting married, after all."

"Parents know best, don't you know that? There's many a slip 'twixt the cup and the lip."

Although it killed him to admit it, Selby was honest enough to acknowledge that one of the things he most admired about Doris was the respect she had for her parents. Despite this, he asked, "Are you saying they still don't trust me? After we've finished giving all the lobola they demanded?"

"I said no such thing."

Nevertheless, they both understood where her parents were coming from. The indaba of marriage negotiations is never over until the courting pair have exchanged their vows.

"I suppose I'll survive," Selby said, sighing. "And anyway," he said, visibly cheering up, "it won't be long now."

"Two short months."

"Woza, December!" Selby shouted, holding his arms high in the air in a warrior's victory salute. He jumped out of bed and into his jeans, grabbed Doris and kissed her soundly, full on the mouth, kissed her long and hungrily.

"Let's go!" he said, coming up for air.

* * *

A clump of youngsters greeted them as they drove into the street in Gugulethu where Doris's parents lived.

"I don't like these laaities hanging around your car," Selby grumbled.

"They're just bored out of their minds," Doris said, making light of it. "What is there for them to do in the township? No cinemas. No sports fields. Nothing at all!"

"Well," replied Selby, "they shouldn't come and do that *nothing* here, near your car."

"You know what they call me?" Doris asked, shaking her head. "Medem."

"I'll wring their scrawny . . ."

But Doris burst out laughing, stopping his tirade. The catcalls and crude remarks were annoying, as no doubt they were meant to be, but she understood their source. She knew these young men and women, had grown up with some of them, knew that like her sisters and brothers they had succumbed to the pull of township living: dropping out of school, becoming parents before they'd quite finished being children themselves and descending into inevitable, hopeless poverty.

"Why bother? I'll be out of here soon enough," she said and chuckled.

"You know," Selby said slyly, "this is another reason for moving in with me."

"Good try!" she said, scrambling out of the car and running round to his side.

Leaning through the window, she hastily planted a kiss on his cheek and skipped toward the gate. Here she turned around and blew him another kiss before entering the yard. Again she looked back, waved and closed the gate.

Only then did he drive away.

15

Monday, 7 October 2002
THEMBELIHLE HIGH SCHOOL, KHAYELITSHA

"Your sister-in-law is on the phone for you, Mrs Zitha," said the secretary coldly. Personal calls were understandably discouraged at the school.

Amanda didn't have to spend her time wondering which of her sisters-in-law it was. First of all, only her brothers' wives ever called her at home or at school. Secondly, of the wives, only Sihle called her at school. Nosizwe never did. And darling Nolusapho, who only ever called her with cheering news, would not dream of disturbing her during work hours.

"Please take her number and tell her I'll call her back," she said. She couldn't leave her class now.

Amanda couldn't remember how many times she'd told Luntu's wife not to call her at school. Yes, she understood Sihle had no phone at home, and no cellphone. She relied on using the phone of the white woman where she worked to make calls. So she called at her convenience, paying no heed to the fact that Amanda had to be hauled out of a class to answer.

At break, Amanda made her way to the office. She recognised the number. Sure enough, it was Sihle. And even before her sister-in-law picked up the phone, Amanda knew it was bad news. Sihle and Nosizwe never thought of calling her when things were going well. Oh no! They only ever remembered her when there was trouble in the family – illness, pressing debt, or a quarrel. Then everyone remembered who to call. PP had soon realised that soft-hearted Nolusapho would run herself ragged if they picked on her, thinking of everybody and what they needed, so he had put a stop to it very early on. That left Amanda.

"Your brother does not appreciate me," Sihle began. "After all the things I've gone through, the hundreds of times I've forgiven him the terrible things he's done . . . Your brother is the lowest of the low. No other woman would tolerate his garbage . . ."

Amanda knew how this would go. Just as she always did, Sihle would go on and on and on, but she wouldn't say what, exactly, Luntu had done. No. The whole family would have to gather to discuss the matter.

Amanda listened impatiently to Sihle. If Luntu wasn't careful, she thought, he'd end up completely breaking the poor woman's spirit. And who would be there to look after him then? He had no idea how dependent he was on his wife. Amanda hoped Sihle would survive whatever abomination her brother had visited on his family this time. Truly, Luntu was a moron. What would happen to his children if something happened to Sihle?

"I can only come after church on Sunday," Amanda said, cutting the call short. "I'll be there."

16 | *Wednesday, 9 October 2002*
DR PATEL'S ROOMS, RYLANDS

The doctor was an elderly Indian gentleman with wrinkled brown skin, grey hair and bushy white eyebrows. As he waved them to their seats on the other side of his desk, he introduced himself as Doctor Patel.

"The procedure is very simple," he began, and smiled at them.

At once Doris felt much more comfortable than when she'd first set eyes on him. The smile had transformed him.

Doris looked at Selby and smiled hesitantly. He was so nervous that he was making her nervous too. Silly, isn't it? she thought. Here's this big man who thinks nothing of getting into a scrum with his burly rugby pals, and he's quivering like jelly.

"I'll give you a little prick on the finger," the doctor went on. "We put the blood on a slide and then we put the slide under a microscope. And you can see the results immediately. There will be one line, or there will be two lines. One line means . . ."

Abruptly, Selby stood up. "Where's the toilet, please?" he asked, interrupting Doctor Patel.

Doris did not for a minute believe that Selby needed to pee. He was just being a big bangbroek.

"Miss," the doctor said after Selby had scurried out of the room, "you want to wait for him?"

"No, thank you. Let's go ahead," Doris replied.

The procedure was so simple, so quick and so painless that by the time Selby eventually returned, Doris had almost forgotten why she was there and was busy laughing at a joke the doctor had cracked.

"Stomach problem?" the doctor asked Selby, standing up and looking businesslike.

Doris noted how the doctor stood, the instrument ready in his hand, but out of plain view. He must get a lot of cowards, Doris thought, smiling encouragingly at Selby as the doctor did the necessary.

Selby's result, like Doris's, was a single line. One line – he was free of the virus.

Selby whooped and danced around, hugging the doctor and nearly squashing the poor man. He was a big man, a fact he seemed to have totally forgotten for the moment, and the doctor had not been a young man when Selby was born. Not even before he was born.

* * *

As soon as they arrived at Selby's flat, he called his mother with the good news. Doris wasn't really listening to the conversation, and it wasn't until Selby had replaced the receiver that a snippet of what he had said came flying back to her: "I was so scared, Mama! What if the result had been positive?"

Doris played his words over and over in her mind – hearing not only the words themselves, but also the sinister meaning they concealed. What if . . .?

Then Selby had had reason to fear he might not ace the test. Selby was not absolutely, positively, definitely certain he was HIV free.

Doris was stunned. She felt so stupid. She had reassured him, calmed him, believing he was nervous, afraid of the needle. How naive of her! Selby hadn't gone to see Doctor Patel as a matter of course. His was a real test! He didn't know his status — and so his fear was genuine, born of excruciating uncertainty. She remembered how certain she'd been of his love. How could she have been so blind?

Is this what had killed Beauty? Blind, unseeing naivety . . .

"Selby," she said, her voice barely a whisper, "tell me I'm wrong. Please, tell me I'm wrong."

"About?" Smiling, he planted a kiss on her lips.

Gently, she pushed him away. "I'm serious," she said, frowning. "What did I hear you say to your mother?"

"That I passed the Aids test."

"And?"

"And what?"

"That's what I want to know. Why did I hear you say, 'I was so scared, Mama. What if the result had been positive?'"

CLICK! Doris heard the key turn in Selby's brain. CLICK! The realisation hit him at the same time as the full implications of his fear hit Doris. What would I have done if he had taken the test first and his test had come out positive? Doris thought to herself. What would I have done, knowing I was almost certainly positive too?

Silence. They stared at each other.

Suddenly Doris began to shake. "Oh, God! God!" she cried. Blind panic made her voice shrill.

"I'm clean, Doris. Isn't that what you should be focusing on? Shouldn't we both be happy about that?"

Doris took a deep, deep breath. "Get out of my sight, Selby!" she yelled. "You lied to me. If you had reason to be scared you might be HIV positive, then you lied to me, Selby! Lied to me!" she cried out despairingly.

"Doris, I can explain . . ."

"Selby, how can you explain making me take chances I had no idea I was taking?" she asked, interrupting him.

"It wasn't like that!"

"If my memory serves me right, we were both virgins when we started out."

"Doririe wam!"

But Doris continued as though he hadn't spoken. "Selby," she said, "why would you ever doubt your status, unless you had slept with some other woman between when we started and today, the day we took the test?"

Selby hung his head, but could not answer her.

Tears trickled down her cheeks.

Selby was stricken. "I can explain," he ventured.

"Know what?" Her voice was barely more than a whisper. "You have nothing to say that I want to hear!"

"But, Doris, why is everything always about you?"

"You have killed my trust in you."

"What's your idea of trust? And where do you get all these bourgeois ideas anyway? I didn't think I was marrying a middle-class white chick!"

Doris narrowed her eyes, grabbed her things and stormed out, banging the door behind her as hard as she could.

Selby came running after her. "You don't have your car here. I'll drive you home."

"No, thanks!" she said, without a backward glance.

He watched helplessly as she stalked straight towards Main Road, flagged down a taxi, leapt into it and slammed the door shut.

Noisily, the taxi revved and took off.

Then, abruptly, it stopped and the driver began to reverse in his direction.

His heart leapt. She was coming back.

The door opened, and out popped Doris's head, her face twisted with fury.

The blur of a flying fist. A yell: "Here, catch!"

Reflex action. Instinctively, he reached out a hand and caught the still-warm ring.

He watched the tail-lights of the taxi glowing red till they disappeared.

The FFF badly needed something to make them feel better. Doris and Cordelia were both in bad shape. Doris had broken off her engagement to Selby, and it was more than a week since Vuyo had left Cordelia. Yes, Edith and Amanda had stuck to their guns: no test, no sex! They had followed their convictions, but the others knew it had not been easy for them. A feel-good gig was surely just what the doctor had ordered.

They placed their orders (they were at Nourah's, a little café big on tasty titbits), and settled back.

Without discussing it, all eyes turned to Edith. Because she seemed even quieter than usual, the others just felt she had to go first. But Edith just shrugged.

"How have things been with you?" Doris prompted.

"I don't know what to make of it. Luvo is behaving very strangely. He is either sullen and will not say a word to me, or he is ranting and raving, saying the most bizarre things I have ever heard."

"Such as?" Cordelia asked.

"Oh, he talks about the lobola he gave to my family. He asks me if I want to wear the pants. He wants to know if I want to be *his* husband . . ."

"What do you say to that?" Doris wanted to know.

"What can I say? I just look at him and keep my thoughts to myself. Since when have I ever laid down the law in that house, that is what I would like to know. Never mind wearing the pants."

Now that Edith's predicament was out in the open, the FFF's thoughts turned to Amanda and Zakes, who were, in Amanda's own words, "inching towards some kind of reconciliation".

"Meaning?" demanded Cordelia, all suspicion. "I hope you're not giving in."

"Of course not," Amanda replied. "Why would I do that?"

She didn't even want to *think* how close she'd been to giving in, never mind confess it to her FFF sisters.

"I don't know," said Cordelia. "L-U-V!" She shuddered.

Amanda sighed. "I wish Sihle had your courage, Cordelia."

"So that . . .?"

"So that I didn't get summoned to family indabas because of her husband's misdemeanours," huffed Amanda, clearly irritated. "The whole tribe is meeting again this coming Sunday."

"That's tomorrow," Doris pointed out.

"So it is." Amanda nodded. "I know he's done something bad again," she said. "If this were good news, Ma or Tata would have called me."

"Good luck!" said Cordelia.

"I'll need it. I've had it up to here with those two younger brothers of mine." She slashed her index finger across her throat. "What that poor woman, his wife, has to suffer is beyond human endurance."

Their orders were served. As they ate, Luntu's inexplicable behaviour was uppermost in Amanda's thoughts. She recalled Mrs Mazwi's words of warning at Lungile Sonti's funeral. What would it take to make people wake up and change their behaviour?

Amanda sighed. Aloud, she said, "What I want to know is why women stay with men who do all this crap? Why stay with men who disrespect them?"

"What do you suggest they do?" Edith asked.

"Leave the louts!" Amanda cried.

"Not always easy to do, my dear . . . not always easy," said Doris. "More often than not, these men are the women's sole source of food and rent, not to mention clothes and school fees for their children."

"And the identity of many a woman is so tied up with her husband's, she wouldn't know who she was without him," Edith said.

"Herself!" said Cordelia, her voice rising slightly. "What would be so wrong with that?" She paused, staring at the others. "The love the African man has for children is in *making* those children, not *raising* them. Oh no! When it comes to raising the children, he does the disappearing act. Look around you. Look at the army of women leaving their homes every morning to go and slave in other women's kitchens. Do they look like they're doing that for pin money? These women work so that their children can eat, so that they themselves can eat."

She paused, challenging them to contradict her, but none of her friends were so unwise as to take up the challenge.

"So don't tell me," she continued, "that her identity is tied to her husband's!" Abruptly, Cordelia stopped. "Don't look!" she whispered, her eyes widening in disbelief. "You will never ever guess who has just walked in with . . ."

Of course, at that, the neck of each one of the other three FFF screwed itself around – they could no more not look than they could stop breathing.

And there was Mr Magama, the principal of a township high school and a deacon in his church. Clinging to his arm, as though glued to it, was a girl who couldn't have been one day older than sixteen. She wore a top so low-cut one saw much more than cleavage, and the wisp of a skirt that she was wearing was so short her panties peeped out with each step she took.

The waiter led the pair past the FFF table. Mr Magama gave the women, whom he knew quite well, a curt nod.

The ill-matched couple reached their table, and the gentleman adroitly unglued himself. Next, he pulled out a chair for the lady. The FFF watched with great amusement as she daintily perched herself, and he pushed the chair back in with the care of a mother pushing the pram of a newborn on her first day out of the house. Finally, when he'd satisfied himself that his companion was comfortable, he took his own seat.

"His wife?" asked Edith in a soft, awe-filled whisper.

"Ii-ishh!" Cordelia sneered. "Not his daughter, either!"

The four women cast surreptitious glances, but refrained from discussing Mr Magama and his yanga-yanga until they were sure the two were comfortably installed and sufficiently occupied with each other not to pay too much attention to their surroundings. People somehow always have a way of telling when gossip is about them. So the FFF waited a few minutes.

Then Cordelia continued right where she'd left off: "Any time you see an African man hovering, all soft, solicitous concern for the woman with him, you can be quite certain that that woman is not his wife!" She spoke with vehemence.

"And I was thinking of getting married?" Doris said, forcing out a dry, sad little laugh that ended in a cough.

* * *

Amanda had to admit, avoidance was no longer an option she cared to pursue. "No test, no sex" was all very well as a slogan, but living it was damn hard. What she couldn't understand was how Zakes was managing the drought. Did he hope to wear her down, believing that sooner or later she would succumb? Well, she had had enough. Her need seemed to have grown with her loss. Beauty's death had opened a hunger in her she had not known she harboured. What to do? Amanda made a vow to herself to take things in hand. Seduction – there was no other way to describe what she was planning. If she was honest with herself, she intended seducing her own husband. Amanda gave a little laugh, light as that of a girl contemplating her first date. For the very first time she would try to *seduce* Zakes into seeing things her way, instead of going at him as though she were a drill sergeant working a raw recruit. And what was wrong with that? What was wrong with a faithfully married wife seducing her own husband?

Amanda spent that afternoon sprucing up the house. She started with the bedroom, changing the linen and spreading a galaxy of rose petals from the garden over the crisp white sheets. She took vases from the kitchen cupboard and filled them with flowers, again from the lush garden she enjoyed but didn't use nearly enough. She put two of them in front of the French windows, and another, a small vase full of violets, went into the bathroom. The sweet scent of honeysuckle made the air in the bedroom light and delicious. If only she'd thought about it earlier, she would have stopped at her parents' house and asked them to keep Zingisa for the night. Oh well, never mind, she told herself. Do the best you can. In any event, she reminded herself, by the time they get home Zingisa is usually so tired he's asleep as soon as he has eaten.

Amanda was quite pleased with her handiwork. She splashed a whole dollop of lavender essence in a tub of hot water and soaked herself, reading *The Way It Was Meant To Be: Essential Reading for Romantics of All Ages*. She had no illusions about what the night ahead had in store for her. It would be tough, but she was a tough lady and she'd made up her mind to use all her wits to march her marriage forward in the right direction.

* * *

As usual, Zakes was late. He shouldn't have been out this late with Zingisa. How many times had she told him that?

Amanda told herself to stay calm. She hadn't gone to all this trouble just to wreck it on the issue of her husband's punctuality or lack thereof.

Finally, she heard the car come to a stop in the garage. She sprang up, dabbed perfume at her throat and between her breasts. Then she went to open the door.

Wearing a huge smile, she stood and watched the two men in her life walk towards her, and her heart welled with love. "Welcome home!" she sang out.

"Huh?" grunted Zingisa. "You look like a lady."

Amanda smiled and ruffled his hair.

Zakes just stopped. Stopped dead in his tracks. The inner glow she felt, enhanced by some subtle make-up, had made Amanda radiant.

Quickly, Amanda led her husband and son into the house – into the study, which was lit, past the bedroom, which was not, down the passage and into the rest of the house. She didn't want Zakes seeing what she had done with the bedroom. Now was not the right time. The moment had to be perfect.

By the time they reached the kitchen, Zakes had recovered. "You smell nice," he whispered to Amanda.

"And I love you too," she said, giving him a wink.

Zingisa was lively, with lots of stories to tell her. But as he prattled on and on, Amanda's responses caused him to ask: "Mama, are you trying to get rid of me?"

"Why?"

"You're not listening!"

"Sorry, darling, I guess Mama is just tired tonight."

"I'm not!" he countered, but his eyes told a different story.

Amanda humoured him a little and was grateful when, eventually, he succumbed to sleep.

Finally, she and Zakes were alone. Pretending a nonchalance she was far from feeling, she left him reading the newspaper in the living room. In the bedroom, she slipped into a pretty little number she'd picked up from Yvette's on the way back to Muizenberg. The brownish berry colour turned her skin a soft butter-yellow.

"Can you come and help me here, Zakes, darling?" she called out softly from the bedroom door.

Absent-mindedly, Zakes looked up from his paper. Immediately, his eyes lit up and, throwing the paper to the floor, he scrambled out of the chair and towards the statue of grace he beheld. "Oh my God!" he gasped. "'Manda!"

That was all he managed to say. And that was all Amanda wished to hear at that moment. As he reached her, goddess Amanda took him by the hand and led him into the bedroom. Her mind had galloped ahead, her heart thundering against her ribs so hard that she unconsciously massaged her breast to slow it down.

Zakes's eyes rolled in their sockets with anticipation. "Mama Ama?" he whispered.

There was no mistaking the desire choking him. Desire sparked by memories of the good times they'd had together before the onset of the cold war.

"Always," she said, as they fell into each other's arms and kissed deeply.

For once, he was not drunk, and this pleased her immensely. She took him by the hand and led him closer to the bed.

"What's up with you?" asked Zakes, a look of pleasant surprise on his face.

"I miss my husband," Amanda whispered demurely. "Anything wrong with that?"

She started to undress him, her eyes locked with his, her lips glistening in the subdued light.

"I'd forgotten how good it is to kiss you," Zakes said, his voice hushed with yearning.

A deep, throaty chuckle was her only response as she drew closer to him once more.

Again they embraced. This time, they fell onto the petal-covered bed.

"I want this to go on for ever," she whispered in his ear, nibbling at the warm lobe.

He groaned. And reached for her.

"You know," she said sorrowfully, "we can only go so far."

He tensed.

"I'm sorry."

He went limp. Then he seized her and held her fiercely. "But why, Mama Ama? Why are you torturing me like this?"

"Oh, sweetheart," she said tenderly, "I want both of us to live long enough to play with Zingisa's children. Don't you?"

"Of course I do," he said, roughly. "You know I do!"

"We can have play-sex," she said, her hand softly brushing against his manhood.

Zakes groaned aloud.

Her heart lurched. She bit her tongue until she tasted salt.

But if her need was urgent, his need was driving him out of his mind. He pleaded, he scolded, he cried. But Amanda would go only as far as Amanda would go.

He hugged her close, skin to skin, her pelvic bones crushed against his as her teeth bit into his lower lip and sent shivers down his spine.

"Let's do it," he said resignedly. "Let's go and take the test tomorrow!"

Tomorrow was Sunday and, except for emergencies, most doctors' offices were closed. But Amanda wasn't going to argue.

She nodded, and hugged him tighter still.

18 | *Sunday, 13 October 2002*
MUIZENBERG

Zakes woke up before her. Humming softly, he made Amanda breakfast. He knew she would be going to church, so he served her breakfast in bed. Tray in hands, he stooped and kissed her softly.

Her eyes flew open. She smiled. "Let's go to the terrace!" she suggested.

She knew how much he loved to eat breakfast there – or used to, when they did things like that. It had been a while. She'd be late for church, but what the heck! God would understand.

The terrace, just outside their bedroom, overlooked both the swimming pool and the vlei. There they fooled around, spooning yoghurt into each other's mouths – apparently, half a loaf was better than no bread at all, and Amanda began to entertain thoughts of the sweet taste of a full meal, complete with dessert!

* * *

"You coming with us to church?" her father asked innocently.

Absent-mindedly, Doris nodded.

"Anything you want to tell us, your mother and me?"

She looked up.

Then her father spoke, asking her question after question. Gently, in his roundabout way, he let her know that they knew.

Doris had not told her family about the break-up. But when her father said, "Daughter, we are puzzled, your mother and I, that you seem to do so little in preparation for your wedding . . ." she knew beyond any doubt that they knew.

She had never told a lie to her father, and the thought of doing so now grieved her. Her father quickly put her out of her misery. "I bumped into Mkhwenyana in town, two days ago," he said.

So he definitely knew.

"What did he tell you?" she asked.

"What you should have told me."

"I am sorry."

"We all make mistakes," he said, looking at his daughter. "I just hope you know that you are not above making mistakes yourself."

It was his way of asking her to think of forgiving Selby, she knew.

* * *

For once, Amanda could leave immediately after the church service. There was no meeting of any of the numerous committees on which she served. She was grateful. She always felt self-conscious making apologies when she couldn't stay for meetings – as though her time was more valuable than that of the other members of the congregation.

Today, however, she could go straight to her parents' home. Amanda hoped the meeting would start on time. She was eager to get home early enough to begin weaving her magic again. Why stop now, when she'd finally got Zakes to agree to go for an Aids test? Amanda was so happy, even the prospect of the tiresome family meeting couldn't take that away from her.

"Molweni nonke aph' ekhaya!" she hailed all present.

"You're early," said her mother. "Will you join us? We're about to have lunch."

Amanda took the apron her mother handed her and went to the kitchen. Her two younger sisters-in-law – Nosizwe and Sihle – were there, getting ready to dish up for the family.

"Need some help?"

"No, sisi," said Nosizwe, "we're managing. Why don't you go and amuse your brothers?"

"Amuse Luntu?" Sihle burst out. She sounded grouchy. In fact, Amanda couldn't remember ever seeing Sihle in such a foul mood. The woman was usually so amicable, given what she endured.

Amanda elbowed Nosizwe aside and took over from her. She wanted a minute or two with Sihle. It would help if she could get some idea of what was afoot before the meeting. She had called her mother earlier in the week, hoping to get some inside info, but all Mamndaweni said was, "Oh, it's the usual complaint from your youngest sister-in-law. That one is forever complaining. We named her wrong, we should have called her Nokhompleni!"

Amanda had not even bothered to set the record straight. In her mother's eyes, women simply endured the vagaries of married life – and did so with their mouths shut and smiles painted on their faces. Men were men and would do what men had always done, since the beginning of time. Mama was beyond changing. So Amanda did not waste time trying to do the impossible. But she felt a word with Sihle was called for.

Sihle understood what had happened – her mother-in-law had withheld the information to shield her son from Amanda's scolding – but just to be sure, she asked, "Mama didn't tell you?"

"No," said Amanda.

"Uyawamithisile! He made someone pregnant – again!"

Compassion for her sister-in-law filled Amanda. Poor Sihle! How could she go on suffering like this?

"Last week," Sihle continued, "this girl, a schoolgirl, came and dumped the baby at my house!"

"Did whaaat? What baby?"

"Luntu's baby. This girl wants to go back to school, and her mother refuses to look after the baby."

"So she brought the child to you? How old is this girl?"

"The mother or the baby?" asked Sihle. "The girl is about sixteen, I guess. The baby is a month old tomorrow."

"My God!" Amanda gasped.

Sihle had a baby herself – a baby whose first birthday was coming up.

Amanda shook her head sadly. "I don't know why you put up with Luntu's stupidity!"

"Why do you put up with *your* husband's?"

For a minute, Amanda was totally lost. Then she saw that in her grief, her understandable anger, Sihle had confused matters. Yes, she sometimes did complain about Zakes. No marriage was perfect. But they were talking infidelity here, exposure to Aids. People who used condoms didn't get their partners pregnant!

"I hope you didn't take the child?" she said.

"I had to. She said if I didn't, she'd take my husband to the courts."

Sihle was always fighting for Luntu's wages, fighting to ensure that she and her children got some of his money.

Again, Amanda said: "I still don't know why you don't leave him!"

But where could Sihle go? Poor and uneducated, she couldn't see a life without the support her husband provided, tenuous as it was.

Sihle was talking on and on.

"Mmhh," murmured Amanda. "What were you saying?"

"You think because yours only has two children outside, you're better?"

"I whaaat?" gasped Amanda.

Immediately, Sihle retreated, her eyes darting all over the place. "Forget it, sisi," she muttered, and tried to slink from the room.

But Amanda grabbed her by the wrist, forcing Sihle to face her.

She heard herself laugh, although she had no idea what was so funny. "What do you mean?" she asked in a voice she did not recognise.

"What do you mean, what do I mean?"

Cornered, Sihle grew bold. There was nothing for it but the truth. And although she would have been the last to acknowledge it, even to herself, there was an element of satisfaction – even glee – in seeing Amanda, who gave so much advice to others, having to deal with the same problems so many of them faced. "You do know Zakes has two children, don't you?" Sihle asked, seeing the look of genuine bewilderment on Amanda's face.

"Zakes has what two children, Sihle?" Amanda asked.

"Zakes. Your husband. I thought . . . Oh my God!"

Suddenly, Sihle began to cry, the enormity of what she had just done hitting home. She began to wail so loudly that Mamndaweni came into the kitchen.

"Who has died?" she asked in a querulous voice.

"I thought she knew! I honestly thought she knew! I swear, I wouldn't have told her if I didn't think she already knew!" Amanda dimly heard Sihle explain.

None of this made any sense to Mamndaweni, however. "Again I ask, who has died?" She could see that her own daughter was deep in shock – ashen-faced and trembling.

"Mama, I'm sorry, but I told sisi about Zakhi and Zandi," Sihle finally blurted out.

Silence fell.

"Oh, Sihle," said Mamndaweni in a low voice full of disdain, fear and a little anger. "You know just how to destroy a happy family. You are no different to a witch – igqwirha." She turned to her daughter. "Amanda," she began, "your husband is a good man. He has made a mistake and –"

So they'd all known! They'd known all along!

"You don't say!" Amanda hissed, interrupting her. "What does a bad man do? Cook his wife for dinner?"

"You're not going to throw everything you have away just because a few common bitches . . ." her mother began, fuming.

Amanda had heard enough.

She stormed out.

* * *

Of all the people Doris had expected to call her after church, Selby's mother, Mama Silwa, wasn't one of them. She had never, ever, called her before, keeping her distance instead, as tradition demanded, until her son would be married to this young woman. So Doris was quite taken aback to hear from her.

Of course! How stupid of her not to have thought of it herself! Her parents would have felt obligated to let Selby's mother know – one mkhozi to another. They must have called her in East London.

Doris was glad the woman couldn't see her face. She'd never been good at lying, or even dodging questions. And right now, Selby's mother was asking her blunt questions, wanting to know why she and Selby hadn't told her about postponing the wedding.

"And why are you doing that?"

She knew perfectly well what this meant, but instead of answering she played for time. "I don't understand," she said.

"No, it is I who should be saying that," Mama Silwa said. "Please call me when you are ready to talk. Don't make me wait long."

Doris promised that she would not.

* * *

The phone was ringing as Amanda opened the door. She let it ring. It might be Zakes, and she simply couldn't face talking to him right now. What she wanted to do was wring his neck. She'd known she'd most probably be home before him, since she had not stayed for the family meeting. She just hoped he didn't get wind of what she had finally discovered

128

before he headed home. She wouldn't put it past her mother to call Zakes on his cellphone and let him know what had happened.

Three hours later, Zakes had still not come home, and neither had he called. So Amanda knew he knew she knew. But she certainly wasn't calling him. If he was waiting for her to call him, he could wait till kingdom come. She didn't trust herself right now. Didn't trust what might spring out of her mouth. Although, what she could say to Zakes and then regret, she couldn't comprehend. What, out of her mouth, could be worse than what he'd done?

Then she heard the car. Zakes's car. The sound was unmistakable. Amanda gathered herself into a secret space inside of herself. And waited.

But it was her brother Luntu who stepped through the door. He had brought Zingisa home. Apparently, Zakes wasn't planning on coming home that night.

She gave her brother a silent reception. He was an accomplice.

Luntu waited till the boy was out of earshot before he started babbling about his wife's stupidity. What business of Sihle's was it to blab about this whole thing? Amanda turned her heart to stone and said not one word in return. If he was there to see how she was taking the betrayal, he could make up his own mind about that. Luntu hung around for a few minutes, but seeing that nothing he said moved his sister to utter a single word, he gave up.

But as he was leaving, Luntu finally answered the one question Amanda was dying to ask. "Man's too scared to come home, Ama!" he said, obviously hoping to provoke her into some kind of response.

Amanda just shrugged. Nothing she could do to Zakes could be even half as bad as what he had done to her and her child – to their family.

But Luntu was the last person on earth she wanted to discuss that with. So, she merely shrugged and held the door open, letting him out. She gently closed the door and turned her attention to her son.

"Want some Milo?" she asked.

"No."

"No, thank you!"

He was quiet.

"I said something?"

But he replied with a question of his own: "What's wrong?"

"Wrong?" Even before Zingisa's eyebrows shot up, Amanda was already telling herself how stupid she sounded. However, once you start off on the wrong foot, it is very difficult to change course midstream. "Why, nothing is wrong," she finished lamely.

Zingisa gave her a sharp look. "When is Tata coming home?" he asked.

That brought unexpected tears to Amanda's eyes. She grabbed her son and hugged him as tight as tight can be. "I don't know," she said. Then, furiously, she wiped away the tears. "But he'll come home sometime, darling. He'll come home. I just don't know when."

It was very late that night when Amanda finally left Zingisa's bedside and dragged herself off to bed, a host of unanswered questions in her heart.

19 | *Wednesday, 16 October 2002*
AFRICA CAFÉ, 108 SHORTMARKET STREET

The Africa Café in Shortmarket Street, away from the centre of town, was Selby's favourite spot. He had often taken Doris there. Tonight, thanks to his mother's intervention – insistence, really – here they were again. However, unlike the other times they'd been here, they now sat awkwardly across from each other, painfully aware of the gap separating them.

"Thank you for coming," Selby said.

She didn't know how to respond.

"I am lost, really lost, without you."

"I miss you too," Doris admitted reluctantly.

A flicker of hope rushed into his eyes. How long did he have to wait before she'd consider getting back together? Selby asked.

Doris said she didn't know. In her heart of hearts, she didn't know if she ever wanted to resume the relationship. Would she be able to trust him ever again? Had there been only the one woman, the one and only time, as he claimed, or had there been other times, and other women? Doris tortured herself with these questions – questions she knew perfectly well would never have conclusive answers. But she also admitted to herself, privately, that she still had feelings for Selby. She had definitely not moved on. What is more, she fervently hoped he hadn't either. But she wasn't going to tell him that – at least, not right now, not tonight.

He couldn't keep her at the restaurant all evening. Therefore, much against his will, Selby drove her home. They promised to meet again, soon. For most of that drive they were silent, each filled with regrets and painful thoughts.

* * *

As Doris and Selby drew up in front of her house, she knew something was terribly wrong. A horrible screaming assaulted her ears, and it was coming from her home.

Selby scrambled out of the car, asking her to stay put while he went in to find out what the matter was. But Doris ran in right behind him.

The screams were those of a neighbour, Mrs Nanto, who lived two doors away.

Her daughter had been raped. Gang-raped. She had come to Doris's house because they were the only people in that whole long street with a land line. The rapists had made off with, among other things, the cell-phones of the entire family.

Selby wouldn't hear of leaving. He insisted on spending the night with Doris's family. Insisted on staying even though her father assured him that they were safe, that they could look after themselves.

The next morning, Selby refused to go to work. Instead, he got workers to come and install burglar bars and security gates at the house. Only then – and reluctantly – would he leave Doris in her father's house.

When Doris told the group how Selby had held the fort, refusing to leave until he was sure her home was secure, Edith was deeply touched. "And this is the man you are having second thoughts about marrying, Doris?"

"You read too many romance novels, Edith," said Cordelia, laughing.

Edith and Amanda joined in the laughter.

"But I take my hat off to him!" Amanda said.

"You're right, Amanda. If Selby came to protect Doris as a friend, then he is a real man," Cordelia said, turning serious. "We need more men like that."

"Coming from you," said Edith, "that's a huge concession. You've made me believe all men are God's error in creation."

Cordelia shook her head. "I see the hurt in my children's eyes now that Vuyo has removed himself from them. They miss him terribly, and I can't make a substitute and give it to them."

Edith grimaced. "Well," she said, "mine will be singing the same tune soon, if things don't change."

She went on to explain that things had gone from bad to worse in her home. Luvo was worse than cantankerous.

"Thank God, he's taken to staying out late, either working in the office or visiting his friends, but the children miss their father . . ."

Suddenly, Amanda cupped her face in her hands. For a long moment, there was absolute silence.

Finally, Amanda said, "I have also become a single parent." Her usually strong voice shook.

Another silence, brief, followed.

"Come again?" Cordelia said.

Then, as the others listened incredulously, Amanda explained the happenings of the past few days. When she was done, the other women were silent again, each mulling over what she had just heard.

Amanda's FFF sisters did not quite know how to console her. The revelation of Zakes's duplicity had hit them hard.

Eventually it was Cordelia who summed up the feeling of despair that had settled on the group. "Are we all going to end up as single parents?" she asked. "That is no way to raise children."

"Oh no!" Edith cried out. "I'm not."

A stunned silence followed this vehement rebuttal. Then Amanda asked, "How can you be so sure?"

"Especially after what you've told us?" Doris added.

"If we love our children, we must do all we can to remind our men of their responsibilities, mustn't we?" Edith said softly. "We must rekindle what has been extinguished by the cruel fires of history. These men are our sons, our fathers, our brothers, our husbands . . . We can't just give up on them. And if we do, we do so at our peril, at the peril of the entire black nation."

"Dream on!" scoffed Cordelia.

Amanda couldn't agree more. Her hope had always been that Zingisa would grow up unscathed by the immoral behaviour of the men around him, some of whom he was in daily contact with, but recently that hope had faded. What chance of that was there if his own father was just as bad as the worst of them?

But Edith was not discouraged. "Know what? Africanists say that the most revolutionary thing an African man can do today is to love the mother of his children!"

Amanda gave a mirthless laugh. "How is anyone going to make our men do that?" she asked.

She was thinking of the men in her life: not just her brothers, but her cousins, friends, neighbours – and now even her husband! It hurt her that people she loved had colluded with Zakes to make a fool of her. Protecting her, they called it, but for her this betrayal just added to her sorrow. She thought of the African leaders, people in prominent positions, who had whole villages of wives and troops of children. Then she thought of the sprinkling of men, African men, who cherished their spouses and had their children, all their children, with only one woman. Her heart bled that she would never be a woman thus blessed. Damn Zakes!

* * *

As Amanda was driving home that afternoon, her mind turned to the inner turmoil she had tried hard to ignore over the past few days. Her heart ached, that she knew, but she also missed Zakes, which told her she still loved him. Yet she was convinced that she could never again trust him. Whatever they had had was dead, even if not yet buried. And that meant she could never live with him again. Zakes would have to go. Love him as she still did, she'd just have to get over that disease. She was sure she would learn to unlove him . . . in time.

Then she recalled her conversation with Sihle, who was willing to take her husband's illegitimate baby to save him the child support he would have to pay otherwise.

Well, that's not me! Amanda thought to herself. I want to see neither child nor mother. Whatever Zakes has done out there has absolutely nothing to do with me – nothing at all!

She focused her thoughts on the other woman, the mother of the children Zakes had sired outside his marriage. She looked deep inside herself, as honestly as she dared, and was surprised at what she found there. While some women fought with other women over men, she discovered she had no hate in her heart toward her husband's lover. That did not mean she loved her. No. The woman was just nothing to her.

However, when she'd thought this over a little more, Amanda surprised herself once again. She felt something for the children – call it compassion. She couldn't find it in herself to be indifferent, not about Zakes's children – the children of someone she had once loved, someone she still loved. But this made her angrier still. Men who father children they fail to nurture are the scum of the earth. How could Zakes, her Zakes, be just another township he-goat?

But not hating someone does not necessarily mean you love them. Not hating the children did not mean that Amanda was prepared to embark on a mop-up operation. No. She had enough on her plate, bringing up Zingisa and making sure he didn't follow in his father's footsteps.

21 | *Monday, 4 November 2002*

First one week passed, then another, and Zakes stayed away, although there was ample evidence that he often returned during the day for a change of clothing. Although he slipped in and out while she was gone, he made certain Amanda knew he'd been in the house, leaving clues she couldn't fail to notice. Briefly, she toyed with the idea of changing the locks, barring him entry. But she decided against it. It didn't seem to answer any need.

Amanda had not known she was blessed with such patience. In a haze, she went about her daily business. For the sake of her child, she kept up some semblance of normality. She couldn't afford to take a break from her God-given duty of parenthood. But Zakes could stay away till hell froze over; she wasn't going to go scouring the city of Cape Town looking for him. He'd have to come home one day. And she, Amanda, would wait until that day came.

Her worry was Zingisa. She had never thought of bringing him up alone. There was always going to be a father . . . there was always going to be Zakes. Always. Would she manage all by herself?

Then, at breakfast on Monday morning, three weeks after the night

Zakes hadn't come home, Amanda asked her son, "You want to know why Daddy is staying away?" She'd decided that nothing beat the truth.

Immediately, Zingisa looked up and nodded vigorously.

As she looked at her son's face, a fresh pang of regret, anger and anxiety all rolled into one hit Amanda. Zingisa's birthday was fast approaching. The boy was hitting double digits, very soon he'd be a teenager – he needed his father.

"I guess he is afraid of what I will say to him," Amanda continued. "He knows I am angry with him."

"Are you?"

She smiled at him. She didn't want him getting confused. Her anger was immense indeed, but it was also extremely focused – directed at a single target. "Yes," she said, quietly but firmly, "I am very angry with him." She shook her head. "And very disappointed, too."

Zingisa made a great show of eating, but she saw he was only toying with the bacon and eggs on his plate.

She stood up and reached over to him. Across the table, she took his slightly chubby face in her hands. Looking directly into his big eyes, his father's eyes, she smiled brightly. "You can always call him at work," she said. "Early in the morning, before we leave, or just before lunch, those are the best times . . ."

His face lit up.

"Can I, Mama? Can I call Daddy sometimes?"

"Sure, baby!" she said, nodding. "You know he loves you!" She watched a cautious smile steal onto her son's beloved face. "Whatever happens between your father and me, he will always be your father. Remember that! Nothing can ever change that, just as nothing can ever change the fact that I am your mother."

"Can I call him now?"

"Sure," she said. "But make it snappy or we'll both be late!"

She boxed him lightly on the shoulder to show she wasn't angry with him. And again she smiled, her heart breaking into shards for her little boy, whose own heart was breaking – hurt by the careless, unthinking stupidity of the adults who were supposed to be nurturing and sheltering him.

22 | *Tuesday, 5 November 2002*

Neither Edith nor her husband wanted their marriage to deteriorate any further. This became apparent when, out of the blue, Luvo had said, "Can you tell me what, exactly, is happening to us?"

And although Edith knew that his concern had been brought to a head by the phone call he had received from the principal at the children's school concerning the drastic decline in the academic performance of both children, Luvo genuinely wanted to try and work things out between them. If only for the sake of the children.

"Usually," the principal had said to him, "when this happens, it is an indication that something is going on at home."

That evening they had sat down together and had a real talk. And since that day, things had started moving in the right direction for Edith. In fact, things had moved to such an extent that on Tuesday morning she called Amanda to invite her to dinner.

Amanda couldn't remember ever receiving a social invitation to Edith's home before. Not after she got married. Luvo hadn't warmed to the FFF. In fact, he'd been distrustful of the other women, Amanda reminded herself. That Edith had managed to cling on to the FFF, despite strong discouragement from Luvo, showed the power of the group's togetherness.

And now she had received an invitation to dinner – at Edith's. Which she had accepted at once – how could she decline? The only reservation Amanda had was that Edith's dinner party made her weekend a marathon. Too many things happening at the same time. For, earlier that very morning, she had also been summoned by her in-laws to a family meeting to discuss the situation with Zakes. This was scheduled for noon-ish on Saturday. Zingisa's party would take place later that same day. And now she had a dinner party on Sunday. Of course, the one event she wished she could avoid was the least pleasant – the family indaba.

* * *

"Mama," said Zingisa, as they drove back from school.

"Yes, my baby?"

"Can I ask Lwandle and Ebony too? To my birthday party, on Saturday?"

Lwandle was Edith's son, and Ebony was a young girl who'd recently moved to Cape Town from Swaziland. Everybody seemed to adore Ebony and Amanda knew she'd made it to the top of every invite list.

Amanda applied the brakes sharply. "I hope you haven't asked anybody yet," she said, looking at him in the rear-view mirror. "You know I said I'd think about it."

"Have you? Thought about it?"

"Yes, I have –" she began.

"Never mind!" he shouted, anticipating her answer and moving into the seat directly behind her and therefore out of her view.

The problem was not space. God knows, the house had enough room for them all. Food was no problem either. With the fisheries nearby, and Kentucky Fried Chicken and Pick n Pay just around the corner. No, the problem was that the meeting to which she had been summoned by her in-laws might take longer than she hoped. If it did, Amanda would have little or no time to hold a party for Zingisa and his friends on Saturday.

Amanda felt for her son. This was no picnic for him, either. She told herself she would do everything in her power to ensure his life was not disrupted more than was absolutely necessary.

"All right," she said. "You can invite as many of your friends as you'd like."

"Can I? Can I really, Mama?" Zingisa asked. "You're the best!"

* * *

Amanda knew she was biting off more than she could chew. As the day of the party drew nearer, so her anxiety mounted. Finally, she did what she should have done as soon as she had started to worry. She called Edith and asked her if she would mind terribly if they combined the two parties. Most of Zingisa's guests were FFF offspring and would be at Edith's dinner party anyway.

"No, not at all," Edith answered. "Actually, I was going to call you. Luvo and I were talking about it this morning, before work. Why have two separate do's in one weekend?"

Relief flooded through Amanda. She certainly did not want to disappoint Zingisa, and cancelling his party would do just that. "You're a true friend," she said.

"Don't thank me, thank Luvo," Edith replied.

"Luvo?"

"He's the one who came up with the plan to have the party early on Sunday. Soon after people come back from church."

That would give the children, all school-going age, time to get back home and finish whatever homework had not been completed in the course of the weekend.

"Can I ask you something?" Edith asked quickly. "The others don't mind much."

"I'll try not to mind much either," Amanda replied, laughing at Edith's transparent attempt at steering her in the right direction – whatever that was. She didn't think there would be any difficulty, since Doris and Cordelia had apparently accepted whatever Edith was about to propose.

"How about Hamilton?"

"Hamilton?" Amanda asked, surprise in her voice. "What about him?"

"All the other parents will be there."

Amanda saw where the conversation was headed. She had managed to stay clear of the rat until now. However, she supposed, it was probably something she couldn't avoid forever.

"Do as you please," she said quietly. She didn't want anyone saying she had been rude to Edith on the phone. "Do as you please," she repeated, and gently put the phone down.

23 | *Friday, 8 November 2002*
MUIZENBERG

Naturally, Zakes chose the Friday before the party at Edith's to finally crawl back home and show his sorry face. Amanda and Zingisa found him busy pottering around the garden. Had he remembered his son's birthday? Amanda wondered. Maybe that's what had brought him home.

"When last did you water the garden, Zings?" Zakes asked by way of welcome.

"Well, well, well! What brings you here?" Amanda asked lamely as he followed them inside.

"'Manda, we need to talk," he said as soon as Zingisa, beaming from ear to ear, went to put his books away. There was urgency in his voice.

"Talk?" she asked, frowning.

"Please, darling," Zakes said. "Just hear me . . ."

But before he could finish Zingisa came bursting into the room and all hope of talk evaporated.

After that, Zakes wandered around the house – like a lost kitten, Amanda thought, hardening her heart while they went through the motions of hemming the day.

After dinner, they all watched TV. Father and son shared the love seat while Amanda curled up on a cushion on the floor.

At about eleven, Zingisa finally threw in the towel and went to bed.

At once, Amanda headed for the kitchen, where she made herself a very, very strong cup of coffee, piping hot.

"I have failed," she said, coming back in from the kitchen and sitting down on the opposite side of the coffee table from Zakes.

He started. "Please, Ama . . ." he began, his voice so low she had to strain to hear him. "Don't blame yourself. I'm the one who . . ."

She looked him straight in the eye. "Oh, but I'm not blaming myself!" she said, her voice firm.

"I thought . . ." he stopped, at a loss about how to go on.

"A marriage does not fail, Zakes," she said. "It is the people in the marriage who fail. Therefore, I take responsibility for my share of that failure."

She found she couldn't go on. Although she had a lot more to say – and wanted to say it now, once and for all – she halted. Cry was the last thing she would do.

"Two children!" she finally burst out. "What happened? Who is she, Zakes? Who is she?"

"Who –?"

"Don't be ridiculous! Who is the mother of your brats?"

"One is –"

"Oh, my Lord!" she cried, putting her head down on her folded arms and beginning to sob.

She hadn't quite believed it. All this while, some part of her she didn't have any idea existed had harboured some secret hope that it was not true.

But it was true. Two women were involved. Two mothers – two children. Perfect symmetry.

After a while, slowly, she unfolded herself. Looking at her husband, she marvelled at the stranger before her eyes. "How could you?" she asked.

"Please, Ama, forgive me."

"I wouldn't have forgiven your infidelity," she said. "I wouldn't have forgiven you for even *one* illegitimate brat . . ." She stopped and shook her head. "Why am I calling the poor child 'illegitimate'?" she asked herself out loud. "What next? Will I be calling that child immoral?" She stood up, stepped towards him and pointed her index finger at him. "*You* committed an illegitimate, immoral act. And *you* –"

"Please listen, Amanda. I'm so very, very sorry!"

"Sorry won't make your children disappear from the face of the earth."

"Amanda, you go to church every Sunday. You must have forgiveness in your heart!"

"Next you'll be saying I must forget? Forgive and forget, is that it?"

"People learn from their mistakes, Amanda. And, believe me, I have learned my less–"

"Your learning will be too expensive for me."

"Hu-uh?"

"If it costs me my life."

"Marriage is about forgiveness. Wives forgive husbands and husbands for–"

"Not when they are dead, they don't!"

"I don't understand, Ama."

"Listen, Zakes," she said, smiling a mirthless smile. "There are mistakes we cannot afford. Aids or getting infected with the virus that leads to Aids is such a mistake. No one can afford it."

Zakes groaned. He remembered his last night with Amanda and the promise he had made her that night – to go with her to take the test for HIV. But why was she bringing all that up now?

"We can go, Ama. I said we could go take the test. Please . . ."

"Damn right I'm going for the test! Tomorrow, if you want to know. You chose to be reckless with your life, but that choice had implications for me as well, something you seem to have forgotten. And I take exception to that, Zakes. I take very strong exception to being exposed to danger when I had no knowledge of it!"

"But we're married, Amanda. I married you, not the other women! And I love you, you know that. You know I love you!" he cried.

Amanda saw red. Why did men seem to think that telling a woman they loved her gave them permission to do whatever they liked, irrespective of the consequences? Did they think that love miraculously protected both of them from infection? Dear God, she was lucky to be alive. First thing on Monday, she would have an HIV test. She cursed herself. She should have gone for that test the minute she discovered Zakes's treachery.

"I love you, Amanda," Zakes spoke into the silence that had fallen.

"And this love you have for me, exactly what is it supposed to do for me?" she asked calmly.

Zakes looked at her in puzzlement.

"Can your love keep me safe from harm? Can your love cure me of disease, save my life, should you infect me with HIV?" she continued.

"But, Ama . . ." he whined.

"Answer me, Zakes. Please, answer me."

But Zakes wouldn't or couldn't answer.

Angrier at herself than she was at him, she turned on him. "A long time ago, I told you I didn't marry you to be your slave," she said. "You understood that."

Zakes nodded and smiled weakly.

"You grew, Zakes, and I appreciate that." She was silent for a moment. "But I should also have told you that I didn't marry you for you to kill me."

"Kill you? When did I . . .?" Violently, he shook his head. "I never once lifted a finger against you, Amanda, and you know that! Yes, you can accuse me of many, many things" – he stopped and looked at her imploringly before he said – "but not that!"

Amanda nodded her head in the direction of his groin. "That thing dangling between your legs, if or when you poke it into any hole that lets you in, it may come out of there wearing death, spitting disease . . . Disease that could kill me like a thief in the night."

Suddenly, Zakes turned angry. "You never loved me!" he shouted at the top of his voice.

"Obviously not," Amanda answered coolly. "Look how I don't have ten children from ten different men to show you how much I love you!"

24 | *Saturday, 9 November 2002*
NY 12, NO. 205, GUGULETHU

All Zakes's sisters were there, and that was something – usually these in-dabas were male-only affairs. The women were dressed in traditional heavy cotton orange skirts with black braiding above the hem and matching doeks, as if to remind Amanda she was a Xhosa woman – ubhinqile – and married to a Xhosa man – wendile. As if to remind her that there was something called tradition.

Taking this detail in, Amanda went and joined the three younger women in the kitchen.

"Sit down, Ama," Nono said as soon as she walked through the door. "Today, you are the guest of honour!" she continued, pulling her by the hand so that Amanda had no choice but to sit down next to her. "There-fore, you do not work."

Victim of dishonour is more like it, Amanda seethed silently, but she smiled weakly and bit her tongue. Nono was her eldest sister-in-law – umafungwashe – and her word was law. She didn't want to antagonise her before the meeting. Especially as she already knew her husband's family would take his side – not out-and-out, but she had been around long enough to know that in such cases, the family met with a preplanned outcome. More than anything else, Zakes's family would want his marriage to survive. Of course, she, too, had wanted that more than anything else in the world. But not any more. Now, what she wanted was much simpler, and far more important – she wanted to live. She wanted to live till her hair turned grey. She wanted to live till she had earned her wrinkles and Zingisa had children of his own. She wanted Beauty's gift – ukhule!

"How are things in Muizenberg?" asked Nobantu, the middle sister.

Amanda smiled. "Except for the problem that's brought us all here, we survive."

"And what are you going to do, Ama? Are you going to forgive our errant brother?" Nono asked.

"I have forgiven him," she began. "But the marriage is dead," she continued, her words wiping away the smiles that had begun to kindle on the faces of the three sisters.

"But, Ama, you say you have forgiven him. What do you mean then?" asked Nono hurriedly, her words running into each other. "What do you mean, the marriage is dead?"

"If you have forgiven him, then the marriage can't be dead!" Nokhaya, the youngest of the three sisters, added.

"I married Zakes because I loved him," Amanda said. "But there can be no love without trust. Right now, there's absolutely no way I could ever trust Zakes again. How do you trust someone who is prepared to risk your life without letting you know he is doing so?"

"We all make mistakes," Nono began. "Show me any human being who doesn't make mistakes –"

"Some mistakes are unaffordable," Amanda replied, interrupting her. "I can't afford to take risks with my life. It is the only one I have."

"What are you talking about, Ama?" Nono shrilled impatiently.

"You think you'll find a better man?" Nokhaya asked.

Amanda clamped her lips determinedly.

Nono broke out in hilarious laughter. "Ama! Ama! Ama! You think we are growing old married to these husbands of ours because love is still home-baked bread, hot in *our* ovens?"

"Oh no!" Nokhaya blurted out. "We all sit over live coals in our own situations."

All three looked at her and nodded in unison. Marriage is enduring, their eyes said, a woman sticks it out the best she knows how, that is what we do. That is what our mothers, and their mothers before them, did. Stick it out. That is tradition.

Amanda looked away. She was stunned. It was obvious to her that they expected her, like them, to endure, to suffer, to remain married to Zakes. That was the respectable thing to do.

She looked again at the three women, and saw pity in their eyes. With a sinking heart, she saw that they were blind to their own suffering, blind to the fact that they were living lives devoid of appreciation and respect. What kind of existence was that?

Her sisters-in-law were beyond salvation. There was nothing she could do or say that could awaken them to the danger implicit in their attitude. But she'd be damned if she would lose her life for the sake of staying married.

Amanda sighed wearily. "I'm not looking for a man," she said. "I'm looking to save my life."

"What 'save my life' nonsense is this?" Nono asked.

"Aids."

"Yho-o!" Nono gasped.

The women eyed one another and shook their heads in consternation.

An uncomfortable silence followed. Three pairs of steely eyes locked on Amanda.

"What are you doing in here all by yourselves?" asked Nontu, Amanda's mother-in-law, poking her head through the door.

"Just chatting, Mama," Nokhaya said. The quietest of the three sisters, she had not spoken much.

"We don't know when Zakes will come," Nontu continued. "We've been waiting for him for more than an hour now," she grumbled. "I don't understand how people who have watches can't keep appointments." She looked at Amanda. "Daughter-in-law, did your husband say he'd be late?" she asked.

Amanda shook her head. "No, Mama. Not to me, that is."

"If he didn't say that to you, who else could he tell?" she mumbled loudly to herself as she walked away, making sure her mutterings reached Amanda's ears. Nontu didn't believe in not letting people know what she thought of them. Right now, she felt Amanda was wasting everybody's time. So what if Zakes had six children outside their marriage? Was he the first man to do that? Was he the last? Was this a story the world had not ever heard before? No. So why did she want to put his name in the history books? Aargh, these women of today . . . and they call themselves wives!

Amanda read her mother-in-law's thoughts as she walked away. But the disdain that came from Nontu only strengthened her resolve. Well, she would be just as bad, as weak, as stupid as Sihle, and all the women she had ever condemned for staying in relationships that had become toxic, if she went the way they wanted her – expected her – to go.

Zakes was well into a bottle of Scotch by the time Lindile arrived at Pepsi's Shebeen.

"Hoezit, my bru?" Lindile asked.

"Mfowethu, don't ask!"

"I'll tell then, my bru! I won't ask, but I'll tell." Jokingly, Lindile bumped him, shoulder to shoulder.

Zakes grinned and shook his head, but he remained silent.

Lindile wrinkled his nose. "Has anyone told you that you look like a drowned cat today? So early in the morning too, my bru! What's up?"

"I'm going to a family indaba . . ."

"About what?"

"The vrou has found out about the boys, you know . . . I'm fucked up, man. I'm really fucked up!"

"Buy her a ring or a necklace, mfana. Women like that kind of crap. Buy her something like that and give it to her. Make sure you cry long tears when you give her those things. Women really –"

". . . like that kind of crap," Zakes interrupted, finishing the sentence for him. He smiled sadly, and looked up at Lindile. "What crap is that, man? Do you know Amanda?" He paused, again shook his head. "No, you don't!"

A few more regulars joined them and the conversation shifted to other pressing matters, but through it all Zakes continued drinking. He wouldn't even take a bite when it was offered to him.

Some time after lunch, Zakes got up, stretched himself, and yawned loudly. He put a hand on Lindile's shoulder, smiled blearily, and announced: "Let me go and face the music!"

* * *

The whole family was waiting for Zakes. Eventually, a boy of about eight came to say Amanda was wanted outside.

"Daughter-in-law," her father-in-law said as soon as Amanda stepped through the door, "we don't see your husband among us. We wonder how that can be when he was asked to come here, and he said he would." He waited a moment as Amanda took a seat next to her mother-in-law. "We see that before long the sun will be going home. And so we have decided to give you the thoughts in our heads."

Amanda nodded and thanked him.

"We want you to know we have heard your complaint."

"Yes, Tata."

"We thank you for bringing it to us first. And we take it seriously. It is in our tradition to deal with matters of this nature and settle those matters amicably."

He sat down, and his older brother, Uncle Xokolo, stood up.

"Tradition says, molokazana, you go home, back to your house," Uncle Xokolo began. "We will see how best to punish our son Zakes. He may not be here now, but sooner or later he will show up. If not today, then tomorrow, or on another day."

Then he too sat down.

"I ask for the forgiveness of my elders," Amanda said as she, in turn, stood up. "But may I speak?"

"Speak, molokazana, this is your home. You are our child," her father-in-law said.

"I am starting a new tradition," Amanda said, head bowed. "I believe I deserve better. You, our fathers and mothers, should have left us a better tradition. Children should all have fathers as well as mothers. I am angry and disappointed that my husband has children he does not put to bed at night or comfort when they have a bad dream. I cannot respect a man who sows his seed as though it were not his blood, a man who sires children but is not there to father them."

"Daughter-in-law, listen . . ." one of the elders, Tata Zitha, said, trying to butt in.

But Amanda would not be stopped. "I respect you, my elders," she said, "but I will never respect lies and dishonesty. And what Zakes has done has killed the last of the respect I had for him."

"There is your daughter-in-law, fathers of this clan," Nontu said, turning to the men. "Hear her words with your own ears, and bear witness!"

Now Amanda raised her head. She looked at her elders, looked each one of them straight in the eye. "I have forgiven Zakes," she said calmly, "but living with him is something I cannot do. We will go our separate ways from now on."

"That is not forgiveness," spat her mother-in-law.

"In my book, it is!"

An uncle cleared his throat noisily. He had something to say. But just then, a loud murmur, as of a crowd approaching, reached the small court. The murmuring grew stronger and stronger, and the growing noise halted proceedings.

They waited.

"An accident! There's been an accident!" someone shouted in the street.

They heard a police van screech to a halt in front of the house, doors banging and soon after two policemen entered the yard.

Tata Zitha stood up and stepped forward, and the policemen, seeing he was the head of the family, motioned to him to follow them into the street. They stopped just outside the gate, speaking to him in low voices.

A minute later, he was back.

Tata Zitha walked slowly to where Nontu was standing. "Our son," he said hoarsely, placing a limp hand on her shoulder. "A car knocked him down." He paused before going on. "And then it ran away."

He didn't say which son. He didn't say how badly injured he was, but with the infallible foreknowledge of mothers the world over, Nontu knew that Zakes, her eldest child, was dead.

* * *

As custom demanded, the family hastily got ready to receive the hordes that would come to their home. The women grabbed shawls to cover their shoulders and went to the main room, where prayers to receive umphanga were to be said. But the shock had nailed Amanda to the chair on which she sat. Someone tied a doek on her head and threw a shawl over her shoulders, while all around her the women and the children wailed, but Amanda did not utter a single word. Not a sound came from her throat. Her mind was a blank.

In no time at all, neighbours, friends and relatives had gathered, and all furniture was removed from the mourning room, which was then readied for the hastily put-together prayers that marked the formal reception of the news of a death.

However, in the meantime, Nontu's mind had been working overtime. "Daughter-in-law, are you happy now?" she hissed at Amanda, red watery eyes holding back pain.

Surprise jerked Amanda's head up.

"You are the cause of this."

Amanda's hands flew to her mouth to stop the scream from spilling out, but Nontu was not done, not by a long shot.

"His mind was not with him, because of you!" she continued vehemently.

Amanda knew exactly what her mother-in-law meant. Distracted by the domestic dispute, Zakes had failed to pay attention to what he was doing. And that was why he had been knocked down by a car.

Emboldened by Amanda's silence, the older woman unfurled herself from her seat. "You! You! You refused to forgive him!" she snarled, a finger jutting out of a gnarled fist pointing towards Amanda.

Right there and then, Amanda knew that Nontu would never forgive her. She inhaled deeply, then dropped her shoulders as she loudly exhaled, her hands falling limply into her lap. And there, for a moment, they rested. Then, slowly, the fingers curled inward until the nails bit hard on the palms.

Suddenly, Amanda's eyes flew open. They were wide and wild. Head slowly shaking from side to side in vehement denial, she stood up, and then, in the voice of one deranged, shrieked: "Noo-oo-ooo!"

26

The whole house hushed. Amanda had done the unforgivable – screamed at her mother-in-law. To this woman, to whom she should not even raise her eyes, Amanda had raised her voice.

"How and when did I push Zakes in front of a speeding car?" Amanda yelled, seemingly oblivious of those around her.

Nontu dithered. "You . . . if you . . . what I mean is . . ."

"Answer me! Mama, ndiphendule! Where was I when the car hit Zakes?"

Nono stepped between the two women, who were by now standing eyeball to eyeball. "Leave her alone, sisi," she said, taking Amanda by the hand.

"No!" screamed Amanda, wriggling free of Nono's grip. "I will not take responsibility for Zakes getting killed by a car. I won't!"

"Hush," said Nono, again grabbing Amanda by the hand.

Meanwhile, Nontu had recovered a little. "If you had forgiven him," she began, her voice still uncertain, "if you had behaved as a wife ought to behave, he would . . ."

"Mama," Amanda said, interrupting her even as Nono tried to manoeuvre her into a chair, "I can only be responsible for my *own* actions, not the actions of others!"

Then, flinging Nono's hand away from hers, Amanda strode towards the door.

No one called out to her. No one tried to stop her.

Blind tears ran down her cheeks as she reached her car, wrenched the door open, clambered in, and banged it shut. Sobbing, she slumped against the steering wheel.

* * *

Later, Amanda couldn't recall driving to her mother's house that afternoon. Thoughts of Zingisa lent her magical powers. She raced to her mother, with whom she had left Zingisa.

"How will you tell Zingisa such an awful thing?" her mother asked Amanda, once she'd got over the worst of the shock.

In a gesture of utter helplessness, Amanda rolled her eyes to the heavens. She was lucky that Zingisa was out with some friends, and they had time to make a plan before he arrived back at her mother's house.

"I suppose I'll have to do it . . ." her mother continued.

Amanda nodded, too choked to utter a single word.

"Leave it to me, then," said her mother as she put a comforting cup of hot tea into Amanda's hand.

* * *

As soon as Zingisa arrived back at the house, Makhulu asked him into her bedroom, leaving Amanda and her father in the living room. By now, her brothers and their wives were expected at any minute.

In the bedroom, Mamndaweni took Zingisa by the hand, hugged him tight against her ample bosom and kissed the top of his head. Then she took him by the shoulders and held him away from her, as though to see him better. She tried to smile, but her lips wouldn't co-operate.

Zingisa sensed the gravity of the moment. His eyes widened.

"You know how much your Tata loves you?" she began.

He nodded, frantically trying to figure out where this was leading.

"You know he wouldn't want to hurt you?"

Again he nodded, trying to dislodge the frog at the back of his throat.

"Well, my child," said Makhulu, "I have some bad news."

He saw the silvery trail snail down one wrinkled cheek, and nodded once more, not knowing he did so.

Then Makhulu told him the sad news. His father was dead. He had been hit by a car.

"But what if the body is not his?" His voice shook. He was scared.

Again Makhulu took him to her bosom. "Then it would be some other child's father, my darling," she said soothingly, "and we can't wish that on someone else."

He would. Did.

But he shook his head. Makhulu was telling him he had to be brave. His father would want him to be brave.

His father had gone to join the stars, Makhulu told him. "This very night, when you look at the night sky, there will be one star brighter than all the rest. Know, then, that's him, your father. And he will be looking down to see that you know he has not abandoned you . . . that he loves you."

He grew quiet. Makhulu's words had soothed him.

They sat quietly for a moment, Makhulu softly massaging his back while he leaned against her chest. Then, once he had gone really quiet, when even the tears that had rushed out without him wanting them to had stopped, they went back to the living room, where they'd left his mama and tatomkhulu. And there more people were waiting. All his aunts and uncles were there, but the boy's eyes fell on Uncle PP, his favourite uncle. He tore himself from Makhulu's side and went and buried himself in Uncle PP's strong, reassuring arms.

The assembled family went into prayer to receive umphanga. Words of comfort were said. During this time, PP stole Zingisa away and the two went outside. They were there for quite some time, and when they returned, Zingisa's hands were deep in his pockets, his eyes sombre. He was obviously still going over whatever it was PP had said to him.

Finally, it was time to head back home. They drove to Muizenberg in silence. Amanda didn't know what she'd expected, but Zingisa's silence concerned her. Was that natural? Shouldn't he be upset? Or at least asking questions? Why was he just sitting there and saying nothing?

Amanda parked the car, and she and her son went into their home.

Before Amanda could do so, Zingisa switched on the lights and locked the door. Then he turned to his mother. "Well," he said, taking her by the hand. "You only have me now. So I guess I'll have to hurry and grow up." He gave her a bear hug. "So I can look after you."

Amanda gulped as she fought back the tears.

27 | MUIZENBERG

"Damn him!" Amanda swore aloud, flinging her cup down on the hard tiled floor, where it smashed into a million jagged pieces. "If he hadn't been drunk, he might have lived!"

"Amanda!" Cordelia said. "Don't do this to yourself."

Cordelia, Doris and Edith had come all the way to Muizenberg, setting off for her home as soon as they heard the news.

"I thought his having children outside was the limit," Amanda said. "Well, was I wrong!"

In silence, the others listened.

"Now," Amanda sobbed, "now, there can be no reconciliation, ever. He won't be there when little Z goes to the bush. He'll never see his son's children . . ."

"Stop it, Amanda!" Cordelia said, interrupting her.

"You're not to blame," Doris added.

"You won't be the first mother to raise a boy child on her own, Amanda," Edith said. "And not the last, either," she added. "And Zingisa will not be the first or last young man who grows up fatherless. You have brothers, and there could be no better role model for a boy than PP. Count your blessings."

Amanda sighed. "Why aren't all men like my brother PP?" she asked herself aloud.

"Now you're talking!" said Cordelia as a chorus of approval rose up from Doris and Edith. Then silence. They all knew they were wishing for the stars.

Then the others turned back to Amanda. What was she going to do now that Zakes was gone?

"I choose LIFE!" Amanda said without the slightest hesitation. "And all thanks to our dear, dear Beauty."

"Meaning?" asked Doris, curious.

"If I couldn't even trust Zakes," she continued, "where am I ever going to find a man who *will* stay faithful? I don't think I will ever want or need a man again, ever."

If truth be told, Amanda only went to the funeral for the sake of her son. She was still angry at Zakes for leaving others to clean up his mess. One thing was clear: had he not been drunk, the outcome might have been very different.

Of course, she'd helped the family money-wise. Nontu had had to eat humble pie, even if indirectly. She'd sent Nokhaya to Amanda to ask about any papers that might help in burying Zakes. Amanda could have done the township thing – fought his family for the body, claimed it, and buried Zakes herself. Legally, of course, that was her right. But she liked to think she was a well-brought-up African woman. Zakes had to be buried according to the customs of his family. Amanda had no problem with that. And whatever fight Nontu wanted to pick with her, she, Amanda, wouldn't let it cloud her judgement. She would take the higher road. And although her first duty was to Zingisa, she would not neglect his grandparents. She would help them, should the need arise. But while there was sadness in her heart that Zakes was dead, she was not grieving.

She didn't sit with the rest of the family on the dais, but with her FFF sisters. Neither did she cover her face with a shawl. She was no hypocrite.

When Zingisa looked back on this day, she wanted that memory to include her, but she also wanted that memory to reflect the truth. And the truth was that Zakes had not honoured his vows, which in turn left her no choice. She could not honour his memory – or the memory of what they had had, which he had betrayed. She was at the funeral to support her son, not to bury Zakes.

29 | *Saturday, 30 November 2002*
MUIZENBERG

The spade-washing ceremony following Zakes's funeral was held on the thirtieth of November. According to plan, Zingisa was shipped off to his makhulu in Gugulethu the very same afternoon. Amanda took him to her mother directly from the ceremony, held at his paternal grandparents' place. Later that evening, she was having the FFF over to supper at her Muizenberg home.

* * *

After the serious business of eating had been concluded, and they had settled down to dessert, Amanda made an announcement. "I'm going away," she said quietly.

"Away?" asked Edith, clearly startled.

"What do you mean," Doris chimed in, "you're going away?"

"I don't know. All I know is I can't face Christmas . . . can't face Cape Town over Christmas. Not this year. I've had it. Enough is enough!"

"But where will you go?" Cordelia asked.

"Maybe the Wild Coast. I hear it's beautiful there."

"Want some company?" asked Doris, her mind ticking over.

She and Selby had reconciled – the day he had installed the burglar bars at her parents' home had led her to rethink her decision. But as the days passed, she had come to realise that something was still seriously wrong. She didn't understand what was happening to her. All she knew was that she didn't feel ready for marriage. She was not even sure – not any more – whether she ever wanted to get married. Maybe the clean Eastern Cape air might help to clear her fogged-up brain.

"Girl," Cordelia said, her eyes positively sparkling, "that is one great idea you have! If you go anywhere halfway decent, count me in."

Although Vuyo had moved out, he had taken to dropping by the house more and more recently. To see his children, he said. Well, Cordelia figured he could see a lot more of them during the school holidays this year. "Far be it from me to deprive a man of the joys of full-time parenting!" Cordelia said, chuckling as she explained her decision.

Amanda was moved, but cautious. She'd kill them if they led her to believe she'd have their company and then changed their minds at the last minute. Oh no! She didn't want her hopes raised only for them to be rudely dashed when someone failed to live up to her promise. She didn't think she could survive another disappointment.

However, after both Cordelia and Doris had assured her they wanted to come along, she was jubilant. Although she had planned to go alone, having her friends with her would make both the trip and the stay, wherever they eventually chose to go, that much more enjoyable.

Hastily, the three made plans to go to a travel agent. Doris recommended a woman who worked at the Go-Far Travel Agency in Claremont.

Thenjiwe Tandwa had done the bookings for her now indefinitely post-poned honeymoon.

"Very efficient," she said.

"Let's strike while the iron is hot!" Cordelia cried gleefully.

At once, cheer returned to the group. A decision had been taken. There was something to look forward to. In the midst of all the calamities and pain and suffering they had endured, they had held on to each other.

A surge of new energy infused them and with it came an optimism they had not felt since Beauty had died. Hastily, the gathering came to an end. There was a ton of stuff to do before their trip – hitherto unplanned, but suddenly imminent.

Only Edith would remain in Cape Town.

30

When Edith got home, she found Luvo waiting up for her.

"All's well on the home front!" he sang out to her as she walked through the door.

They were on much friendlier terms these days, to be sure, but had not as yet resolved the issue at the heart of their stand-off – that of using condoms till they had both taken an HIV test. But this evening something in the manner of Luvo's greeting, something in the look he gave her, set Edith's heart beating. She felt herself blush.

Hold your horses, Edith, at once, she told herself. There's homework to do before graduation.

But her husband's eyes were all over her. And they were hungry eyes. "I have feelings, tonight," he said lustfully.

As calmly as she could, she reminded him of the unresolved business between them.

"Let me love you tonight," he said as he grabbed her and dragged her into the bedroom.

"No, Luvo!" Clearly, calmly she said it. Repeated it.

That was clear enough, but he didn't even seem to notice she'd used his name, something tradition forbids. A Xhosa wife does not address her husband as though he were her son.

"Baby, baby!" Hot breath on her neck, wet kisses behind her ears.

Edith wanted to scream, but she feared making a noise. That would wake up the children. And they were at the age where they knew things. She didn't want her babies ever to see their parents doing the ugly thing. The boy, Lwandle, was a light sleeper. Where would she hide her face if he happened on them like this? Dear God!

Edith wriggled, pushing Luvo off her and away. However, although seemingly the lighter of the two, he was much, much stronger than she. For a while, the struggle was desperate, both heaving and gasping, and hoarsely urging the other to "Stop!"

When she finally understood that he would not stop, she went into passive-resistance mode. She lay there like a log and let him do whatever.

It was over in seconds.

And it woke up something ugly in Luvo. He cursed angrily: "Dead fish! You make me sleep with a cold, dead fish!"

Grumbling, he disappeared in the direction of the bathroom.

Edith turned on her side, facing the wall. She pulled at a corner of the sheet and wiped herself clean – well, as clean as possible. She was too shocked, too afraid to get up and go to the other bathroom. She felt humiliated. Why had he not listened to her? She had said "No!" Her lips trembled, but her eyes stayed dry.

That night, they slept back to cold back. Or Luvo slept. For Edith, it was a long, dark vigil.

* * *

171

The next morning, a Sunday, Edith laid the table for breakfast and then left. She did not return till after supper, well after supper. And she returned wearing pants, to the loud praise of the children. And all she said, all she would say to her husband, was: "I'm going away for the holidays."

"Going away?" Luvo asked, frowning. "What d'you mean 'going away'? And where did you get those . . .?"

Edith didn't wait for him to finish. "I need to go away and think about what you did last night. And," her eyes narrowed to slits, "don't ever do that to me again."

Was it the set of her jaw? The low and deliberate tone of voice? Those narrowed eyes? Luvo didn't know. But, that evening, there was something about his wife, about Edith, that made Luvo pay attention to her – really listen to what she said. So, for the rest of the evening, he followed her every movement, but kept his thoughts to himself.

That night, Edith slept in a sleeping bag on the floor of their bedroom.

31 | *Monday, 2 December 2002*
GO-FAR TRAVEL AGENCY, CLAREMONT

Edith, wearing pants, was first to arrive at the Go-Far Travel Agency. Cordelia, Doris and Amanda found her waiting there for them.

"I'm coming too," she told them, her voice quiet with determination.

"But . . ." Doris started, then stopped, for Edith was shaking her head.

"That was two days ago."

"But . . ." Doris said again.

Edith, anticipating her query, answered: "He can take care of the children. And if things get too tough for him, there is always his mother. God knows, she's eager enough to be of help. Well, let her!"

"Yes, but what's changed your mind?" Doris persisted.

"And since when do you wear –"

"Pants?" Edith chuckled. "I didn't come here to answer questions," she said, serious again. "Time enough for that later, when we get there. Just take it that I *am* coming with you!"

They were all going!

* * *

The FFF left the travel agency floating on air. Their tickets were booked and paid for.

"Where did I park?" Edith asked herself mournfully.

The other three looked at one another and smiled. Fortunately, it wasn't one of those high-rise parking lots.

When they found her car, they stood in a circle and, eyes bright with unshed moisture, hugged each other tight as tight can be. Amanda remembered Beauty's wish to her on her birthday, four long months before. A smile spreading slowly across her face, she shook herself free from the hug and looked at the other three members of the FFF standing before her. "Ukhule!" she said, to each in turn. "Ukhule!"

Acknowledgements

The Ledig-Rowohlt Foundation, for giving me the opportunity to stay, write and work in the company of other writers – an indescribably inspiring experience. This is where *Beauty's Gift* was conceived.

Andrew Zawacki, a writer I met at Château de Lavigny, Switzerland, for introducing me to the American poet Wallace Stevens.

Thokozile Fezeka Sayedwa, my daughter, for being my first reader and making me believe.

My long-suffering agent, Lisa Erbach Vance, for her unfailing support during the long years of drought.

SINDIWE MAGONA is motivational speaker, author, poet, playwright, storyteller and actor. Her previously published work includes two auto-biographical books, *To My Children's Children* and *Forced to Grow,* two collections of short stories, *Living, Loving and Lying Awake at Night* (Africa's 100 Best Books of the 20th Century) and *Push-Push and Other Stories,* and a novel, *Mother to Mother*, recently optioned by Universal Studios for a film on the life of Amy Biehl.

Magona has also published thirty children's books – in all eleven languages of South Africa. She has been published in the *New York Times*, the *Cape Times* and the *Cape Argus* as well as in magazines. Several of her short stories and essays have been anthologised.

Magona has received, among others, the Molteno Medal (Gold, 2007), the Premio Grinzane Terre D'Otranto (2007) and the Department of Arts and Culture's Literary Lifetime Achievement Award (2007). She also has an Honorary Doctorate in Humane Letters from Hatwick College, Oneonta, New York.

Besides participating in writers' conferences, Magona has given readings and addresses at numerous other international forums, including the United Nations, the Kennedy Centre, the Riverside Church, the Ford Foundation, Temple and Columbia Universities, to name a few. She has received numerous awards in recognition of her work in women's issues, the plight of children, and the fight against apartheid and racism.

Magona lives in Cape Town.